"You wer
I bough

He turned his head and studied her, and saw the lines of strain etched on her face. Tears had dried on her cheeks, the moisture stripped out of them by the sun and the wind, and the salt trails ran down to her chin. His heart went out to her.

"Maisie, I'm really sorry. I don't know what to say."

"You could tell me how," she said, her voice stunned with disbelief.

He stared at her, the flippant reply hovering on the tip of his tongue, and the utter bewilderment on her face stopped it in its tracks. She looked shocked to the core, and James realized that he was dealing with something very much more complex here than simple denial, something that was going to take all his skill and understanding to help her through.

What happens when you suddenly discover your happy twosome is about to be turned into a...*family?*

Do you panic?

Do you laugh?

Do you cry?

Or...do you get married?

The answer is all of the above—and plenty more!

Share the laughter and the tears as these unsuspecting couples are plunged into parenthood! Whether it's a baby on the way or the creation of a brand-new instant family, these men and women have no choice but to be

READY FOR BABY!

When parenthood takes you by surprise!

THE PREGNANCY SURPRISE

Caroline Anderson

READY FOR
BABY!

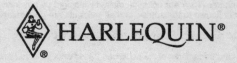

HARLEQUIN®

TORONTO • NEW YORK • LONDON
AMSTERDAM • PARIS • SYDNEY • HAMBURG
STOCKHOLM • ATHENS • TOKYO • MILAN • MADRID
PRAGUE • WARSAW • BUDAPEST • AUCKLAND

ISBN 0-373-03826-7

THE PREGNANCY SURPRISE

First North American Publication 2004.

This edition published by arrangement with Harlequin Books S.A.

® and TM are trademarks of the publisher. Trademarks indicated with ® are registered in the United States Patent and Trademark Office, the Canadian Trade Marks Office and in other countries.

www.eHarlequin.com

Printed in U.S.A.

CHAPTER ONE

'I SEE your new neighbours are moving in.'

'About time. It's been empty for nearly a year.' Maisie lowered the wallpaper sample and peered out of the bedroom window, eyeing the hive of activity below with interest. 'Good grief! Is that a big enough removal van?'

Kirsten, with no attempt at subtlety, was leaning out of the other little window and openly studying events as they unfolded. 'There's some nice stuff coming out of it.'

The cavernous interior of the huge lorry was being systematically emptied by a fleet of bulky, sweating men. It was these contents that were attracting Kirsten's interest, but Maisie's had moved on in a different direction.

Supervising operations as the removal crew struggled with the contents was another man, standing to one side of the drive and scowling from time to time at the clipboard in his hand. No wonder he couldn't remember where everything was to go. The van was big enough to house the contents of a stately home!

'If that lorry was full, they must have been at it all morning,' Kirsten mused.

It was quite possible, if the number of pages flapping around on the clipboard was anything to go by. Maisie had only come back with Kirsten in her lunch-break to let the dogs out and get her friend's opinion on the wallpaper, and it seemed she'd missed much of the action.

Pity. Her eyes flicked back to the man again, scanning his tall, lean frame, checking out the way the sun gleamed on the ruffled strands of his dark blond hair, and her heart did a little shimmy in her chest.

Lord, girl, you need to get out more, she told herself in disgust.

'Oh, that's pretty.'

She gave Kirsten an odd look. Pretty? She wouldn't have called him pretty. Architectural, maybe, but pretty? Definitely not—unless Kirsten was talking about the dog.

'The little desk. It's gorgeous.'

Maisie looked again. Gorgeous? Not by her standards. Sure, the desk was OK, but the dog that had appeared at Mr Clipboard's feet—a delightful golden retriever with floppy ears and a daft grin and a wet, lolling tongue that she'd just bet could lick you for England—now, she was gorgeous, but even she couldn't hold a candle to her master in the eye-candy stakes.

He'd exchanged the clipboard for a huge pot plant, some kind of palm or tree fern, and as he strode towards the conservatory with it, the dog bounced around under his feet and nearly sent the man and the plant flying. He said something to the dog, but whatever it was it didn't have much effect, and after another couple of strides he gave up and put the plant down, ruffling the dog's ears affectionately and laughing.

And it was so infectious. Kirsten could feel the

smile starting deep inside her, and she couldn't take her eyes off him. He was *beautiful*...

'Mmm,' she said appreciatively, and earned her own odd look from Kirsten.

'I thought you didn't like dusty old antiques?'

'What?' Maisie stared at her blankly, then realised her friend was still talking about the furniture. Because, of course, Kirsten was stationed at the other little window and might not have noticed the man from her slightly different perspective.

Maisie, however, had most definitely noticed him, and had to drag herself away. In just a moment...

Which was, of course, too late. He looked up, and for a second she thought her heart was going to stop. He was staring straight at her, his ice-blue eyes hypnotic, mesmerising her so she couldn't break the contact.

Ice blue? He was miles away. Well, not miles, but far enough that she couldn't possibly see his eye colour. And yet she knew it, just as she knew the sun would rise in the east and come in that damned window and shine right in her eyes.

She sucked in some much-needed air and let it out on a quiet snort of disgust. So he was a hunk. So what? There were plenty of good-looking men around.

They just all seemed to be either married or so full of bull that she lost interest in the first few seconds.

'What on earth are you looking at?'

'Nothing,' Maisie denied, moving rapidly away from the window and heading for the stairs, her wallpaper samples forgotten. 'Cup of tea?'

'Mmm. You could take one round to him—he's

rather lovely. No wonder you were showing so much interest. Actually, on second thoughts, give me the tea, I'll take it. Is he single? No, don't answer that, it's irrelevant. I'll just kill his wife. What a scoop— the man *and* his fabulous furniture.'

Maisie chuckled. 'You're outrageous,' she told her friend, then almost stopped in her tracks as another emotion broadsided her. Jealousy? Was that strange urge to trip Kirsten up so she couldn't walk round there *jealousy*? Good grief!

'I'm sure they don't need tea,' she said firmly. 'Much too hot. And may I remind you it was you who started the curtain-twitching. And I believe he is single.'

The last was an afterthought, but Kirsten stopped dead behind her on the stairs and gave an accusing gasp of laughter.

'Well, you sly old thing, you *are* curious!' she said victoriously, and Maisie had to fight the urge to blush.

'Not at all. The builder said something about it, but I could be wrong.'

Actually, the builder had said he couldn't understand why a single man would want to live there, rattling around in a bloody great place like that all on his own, pardon my French, so Maisie had, hoping for further information, but her bleep had gone off and the opportunity for further revelations had been cut off in its prime. If only she hadn't been on call...

'Make lemonade,' Kirsten suggested, going tenaciously back to her passport onto the man's property. 'After all, it would only be neighbourly on such a hot day and I know you've got lemons, I saw them in your fridge. And, anyway, I'm sure you're dying to get a look at all the renovations.'

'It would be interesting. I doubt if poor old Miss Keeble would recognise it, though. It's been torn apart, but I'm sure it needed it. It must be years since the place had any real maintenance. So—lemonade, you think?'

'Absolutely.'

So she made some—a huge jug of it, with the fresh lemons that she'd bought on impulse to go with a rainbow trout and had then forgotten to use. She'd had to buy a net of them, because the single ones had sold out, and there they were sitting in her fridge, as Kirsten had said, needing a good home.

So she made lemonade, brimming with vitamin C and sharp tang and real flavour, and, trailed by Kirsten with a huge box of biscuits given to Maisie by a grateful client, she told Jodie and Scamp to stay and she and Kirsten trooped out of her gate and round and in through his, just as the removal men slammed their doors and drove away.

He was standing on the drive, hands on hips, looking around his garden with satisfaction, and as they approached he looked up and scowled.

Well, no, perhaps frowned was a better word.

She gave a mental shrug and put on her best neighbourly smile. 'Hi. Thought you could all use something cool to drink—it's a scorcher, isn't it? But we seem to be too late for your removal team. I'm Maisie, by the way—I live next door.'

'And I'm Kirsten,' Kirsten said, sidling round her and putting on her best *femme fatale* smile and holding out her hand. 'Welcome to Butley Ford.'

Maisie sighed inwardly and tried not to notice how Mr Drop-Dead Gorgeous ran his eyes—and, yes, they were quite definitely glacier blue—over Kirsten's bare, brown and endless legs and smiled. Still, at least the frown had gone. He shook her hand politely, but then his eyes flicked back to Maisie and the smile changed, becoming...

What? Less formal? Surprised?

Why surprised? There were no surprises about Maisie. Five-four, short unruly dark hair, toffee-brown eyes—she was pretty average, really, so why he was looking at her like that?

He extended his hand to her. 'Hi. I'm James. Nice to meet you. This is very kind of you, but you really didn't need to bother.'

Great. He was going to dismiss them, and now she'd feel a fool, not to mention the wasted lemons. Oh, well, they had started to wrinkle, so it wasn't really a waste, and it just went to show how wrong she'd been about him looking at her—

'Oof!'

The jug jerked and slopped, deluging her less-than-ample bosom with ice-cold lemonade, and she let out a little shriek.

'Sorry, blasted dog's got no manners. Tango, get *down*!'

He dragged the dog off, totally unabashed and still wagging its tail furiously, and then relieved Maisie of the jug and handed her a snow-white and immaculately laundered handkerchief. 'I'm sorry. She just gets a bit excited.'

A bit? Maisie blotted her chest ineffectually and

looked at the mutt with a jaundiced eye. So much for the elegant entrance!

'Is your wife inside?' Kirsten was asking politely, still concentrating on the core business while Maisie just went for damage limitation.

'No,' he said, in a tone that implied he knew exactly what Kirsten was up to and found it mildly amusing. He waited a heartbeat, during which she swore none of them breathed, then added casually, 'I don't have a wife.'

There was a rattle, and the lid was off the tin. 'Biscuit?' Kirsten said, almost as if she was rewarding him for being single, and Maisie nearly choked on her laughter.

His lips twitched briefly. 'Thanks. Look, why don't you both come inside? I don't know if I can find glasses...'

'We won't trouble you—'

'Oh, how nice—'

She and Kirsten spoke at once, and she gave her friend a sharp look that was ignored with a skill born of years of practice.

But James was looking at her, not Kirsten, one brow raised as if he was waiting for her answer, and with a faint smile she shrugged in defeat and trailed them both inside.

The dog, freed by now, was bouncing round their feet barking and grinning and lolloping like a baby— which, of course, Maisie could see she was. Nine months? Ten? She'd be a baby for a good few years yet. Retrievers only seemed to grow up when they got arthritis, and sometimes not even then.

She needed training—quiet, gentle, no-nonsense

training, not people shrieking and grabbing her and turning it into a game, so that she got rewarded every time she was bad.

Hobby-horse, she told herself, and concentrated on not making more of an idiot of herself than she already had.

She blotted once more at her soggy front and sighed. Of course, it would be her thin white T-shirt—the one that went totally transparent when it was wet. She said something very rude in her head and followed James through the door.

They'd gone in the back way—the tradesmen's entrance, her jaundiced little alter ego reminded her—through the old scullery now refurbished with what looked like solid oak units and a huge white china butler's sink big enough to bath an elephant, and into a kitchen that was to die for.

More of the lovely pale gold oak units bracketing a massive white four-oven Aga curled around one end of the room, and at the other end was a huge fireplace with a pair of sofas facing each other in front of it. Between the two areas, in the centre of the room, squatted a vast old refectory table piled high with boxes.

Miss Keeble would have approved, Maisie thought. She'd always regretted not being able to look after the place, and she would have loved the sofas. And so, of course, would her dogs!

Tango, however, possibly better trained than she appeared or maybe just too hot, flopped down on the stone-flagged floor, stretching out her legs frog-like so that her tummy was pressed on the cool stone and dropping her head between her paws with a great big sigh.

'Is that lovely?' Maisie said to her, and the dog wagged her tail lazily and grinned agreement.

'Stupid mutt. Only sensible thing she's done all day,' James said with a weary smile, and scrubbed a hand through his hair. 'The removal men had their own drinks and I've just stuck my head under a tap, so I'm afraid I have no idea where the glasses are.'

'In here?' Kirsten was pointing at a box, and he shrugged and peered at it.

'"Glasses",' he read, and pulled a wry grin. 'Bingo.'

He slit the packing tape with his keys, whipped open the lid and pulled out three tall tumblers. 'That's what you get for having packers—a bit of logic. I would have thrown them in any old box and spent weeks looking for them.'

'There's time for that yet,' Maisie said drily, remembering her own move. 'I've been in my tiny house for three years and I've still got boxes I haven't unpacked.'

'Here.' Kirsten had rinsed out the glasses and filled them with the lemonade, and Maisie took one.

'Please, ladies, have a seat,' James said, waving a hand at the sofas.

Maisie sat, and Kirsten, predictably, took the other sofa. So now where's he going to sit? Maisie wondered, but he didn't. Instead he propped his lean hips on the side of the refectory table and took a cautious sip. He gave a sensual groan that almost made Maisie whimper in reaction, then sighed and drained the glass.

'Oh, bliss. Real lemonade. My compliments, ladies.'

'Thank you,' Kirsten chipped in, before Maisie could even open her mouth, so she simply sighed and took a biscuit from the tin—her tin!—that he proffered, and resigned herself to yet another inch on the waist that seemed determined to grow almost daily. Still, at least she'd got her appetite back after her bug, even if it had taken weeks.

Kirsten, of course, refused a biscuit, but James took one and bit it cleanly in half with those dazzling, almost-too-perfect teeth, and Maisie had to stifle another whimper.

She drained her glass and stood up. 'Sorry, got to go back to work. I hope you don't have too much trouble settling in.'

'I'm sure it will be hell,' he said mildly, and put the lid on the biscuit tin. 'Here, take these back. I can't possibly eat them all.'

'Keep them,' Maisie pleaded, knowing perfectly well what would happen if she took home the opened tin. She was going to have to do something about her weight gain, and the biscuits wouldn't help at all. 'It'll save you having to cook for a day or two.'

'There are some good pubs and restaurants in the area,' Kirsten said, less than subtly. 'I could show you, if you like.'

His eyes flickered with amusement for a second, then went politely blank. 'I'm sure I'll find them when I need them,' he returned smoothly, and held the door so Kirsten had no option but to leave with her. 'Thank you again for your welcome.'

But this time his eyes were on Maisie, and the smile that crinkled them was genuine and warming.

Very warming. Oh, lord.

'My pleasure,' she managed. 'I'll wash your handkerchief and return it.'

'Don't worry about it. I'm sorry about your T-shirt.'

His eyes lingered for a second on the damp, translucent fabric, and the heat mounted. Then his eyes flicked up to hers once more and he smiled again, a polite social smile this time, and closed the door.

Her legs threatening to rebel, Maisie turned on her heel and headed round the side of the house and down the drive, Kirsten beside her chanting softly under her breath.

'Oh, boy. Oh, wow. I'm in love. He is—'

'Gorgeous,' Maisie finished for her. 'I noticed. I wonder what he does.'

'London,' Kirsten said firmly. 'Must be. Something big in the City. He's obviously got pots of dosh. Did you see that new kitchen? I'd die for a kitchen like that.'

'I'd die for the sink in the scullery, never mind the kitchen.'

'Pity we had to leave so soon—I was angling for a snoop round the house. All those priceless antiques—the man must be worth a complete mint. All that and those looks, too. There's no justice. God could have spread it around a bit!'

'I'll share,' Maisie promised, laughing. 'You can have the antiques.'

'In your dreams!' Kirsten retorted, and Maisie thought it was quite likely. It was the only way she'd come within spitting distance of that particular fantasy!

They turned up the lane beside the garden wall and walked up to Maisie's little house. 'You need a gate in the wall,' Kirsten teased. 'Think how handy that would be.'

'There is one,' she pointed out. 'It's covered in creeper, but it's there, from when the Lodge belonged to the house—it used to be the old doctor's surgery, and the doctor lived in the Mount and presumably just nipped through the gate to see his patients. Nice and handy.'

'Mmm,' Kirsten said, her eyes brimming with laughter. 'Perhaps you should dig out your secateurs.'

'Or not.' She checked her watch. 'Just got time to change my T-shirt and then I'll have to go back to the surgery. What are you doing?'

Kirsten laughed. 'Well, I know what I'd *like* to do, but I guess I'm going to come back to town with you unless I want to be stranded. There's an interesting thought…!'

'You're incorrigible. Don't you have any clients to see?'

Kirsten shook her head. 'No, just paperwork and orders and following up a useless builder.'

'Lucky you! I've got a full surgery—stitches out, inoculations, anal glands—I can hardly wait. I've got a follow-up of an intractable itchy coat—what do you bet me it's a wheat allergy and she won't stop feeding the poor dog the crusts off her toast? If you ask me, most pets would be better off without their owners.'

'All except Tango,' Kirsten chipped in with a grin. 'I wonder if he's going to take her to the vet any time soon? Or, better yet, I wonder if he needs any interior design advice? All those rooms—he can't possibly have got them all sorted yet and he'll need the right backdrop to set off his goodies.'

Her eyes sparkled with mischief, and Maisie chuckled. Her friend was relentless.

'Why do I get the feeling he'll get one of your flyers through his door in the next day or so?' she said drily, and Kirsten's eyes widened.

'What a wonderful idea! Maisie, you're a star!'

And Maisie, seeing the futility of setting herself up in competition with the beautiful and sparkling Kirsten when she was on a mission, gave an inward sigh and conceded defeat. Kirsten wanted James? She'd get him, regardless of his feelings in the matter. Of that Maisie had no doubt.

Hot, sweaty, his muscles screaming in protest, James wrestled the heavy mattress onto the old mahogany four-poster and sat down on the end of it to catch his breath. He must have been mad. Try as he might, he couldn't for the life of him remember why moving up here had seemed such a good idea. Why saddle himself, a single man, with a huge house and two acres of garden to rattle around in all alone, miles from all his old friends?

Just having a place to store the furniture he'd grown up with was no good reason, he thought, lifting his head—and there, laid out in front of him on the other side of the window, was the real reason, and they didn't come much better than that.

The salt marshes, dotted with sheep and a haven for birds at this time of the year, stretched away to the left as far as he could see. To the right was the pretty little riverside town of Butley Ford, loved and remembered by him since his childhood, and straight ahead of him a path led enticingly across the marshes and joined up with the river wall where he'd walked all those years ago with his grandfather.

Grandy was long gone, and so, now, were his parents. Only he and his sister were left, and she'd gone off to the other side of the world to sail the Pacific with the new love of her life, leaving Tango with James—'just until I come back'.

If she ever did. She'd already put off her return once, and James had a feeling that the next time he heard from her, it would be to tell him she wasn't coming back at all.

Ever.

He glanced down at the dog, sitting up at the window and staring hopefully out over the new and fascinating landscape. The tip of her tail was wriggling with enthusiasm, and she turned her head and looked up at him hopefully.

He sighed and hauled himself to his feet. He was knackered, and absolutely the last thing he needed was to take the dog for a walk, but she'd been good all day—well, as good as she got—and it was a beautiful afternoon.

He looked out of the other window, the one on the flank wall, and studied the little cottage that was his nearest neighbour. Was that Maisie's? Curiosity stirred in him, but the dog was jumping up and looking hopeful, and his attention was distracted.

He ruffled her soft, pretty head. 'Come on, then,

Tango. Let's go and find that walk I used to go on with Grandy.'

The dog bouncing round his feet, he found her lead and headed for the river.

'Let's go for a run, shall we?'

Jodie and Scamp were at Maisie's heels instantly, tails lashing. Scamp, the springer, squirmed with excitement while she changed her shoes and clipped on their leads, but the elderly lurcher just watched her as if butter wouldn't melt in her mouth, eyes bright in the amber fuzz that made up her coat, then they were trotting along quietly beside her even though they'd been waiting all afternoon for this.

They were good dogs, she thought, and even quite civilised now. Great friends and wonderful company in the evening, and they didn't chatter in the morning either. Maisie hated people that chattered in the morning—and that went double for the cockerel!

They walked down the lane to the end, crossed over to the path that ran between the fields and then followed it to the foot of the river wall, then up the few steps to the top. Once up there, she turned left and broke into a jog, heading inland, and they loped along beside her still on their leads.

It was the breeding season, and she wouldn't trust either of them not to disturb the nesting birds. She had enough trouble keeping them out of the chicken run! Well-behaved they might be. Saints they were not.

And neither was Tango. She came streaking towards them, barking wildly and lashing her tail, and skidded to a halt a few feet away as it if had suddenly dawned on her that she might not be welcome. Her tail was still waving, but she looked much less confident, and Maisie watched as her two dogs checked out the youngster, circling her and sniffing all those important places.

'Sorry—she got away from me.'

Maisie looked up, shielding her eyes from the sun, and found herself only a few feet from a gasping James. He'd obviously been running, and now he was bent over, hands on knees, trying to get his breath.

'You should keep her on a lead—the water birds are breeding, and she hasn't even got a collar on!' It came out sharper than she'd meant it to, and as soon as the words were out, she could have kicked herself.

He glanced up at her, arching a brow, then he pulled a lead from his pocket and dangled it in front of her, the collar still attached to it. 'I tried,' he said, his reproach mild, and she felt a pang of guilt. After all, they were going to be neighbours, and she didn't want to get off to a bad start.

It was going to be difficult enough when he encountered Hector!

She dredged up a suitably apologetic expression. 'Sorry—I didn't realise. It's just that so many people—'

'Don't worry about it.' He was still breathing a little hard, and Maisie crushed the urge to smile.

'Out for a run?' she asked innocently, and he snorted.

'Not exactly. That was all Tango's idea.'

Maisie's lips twitched. 'I bet she thought that was great fun.'

'I'm sure she did.' Hands on lean, jeans-clad hips,

he straightened his shoulders and gave a wry smile. 'Since I seem to be this close to her, I think I might put her back on the lead and quit while I'm winning.'

'Sounds like a plan,' Maisie said, letting the smile show now. 'Of course, if you tightened her collar the birds would be safe and you wouldn't risk a coronary.'

He stared at her for a second, then his mouth quirked and he gave a little huff of laughter. 'Do I look that unfit?' he asked, but she just shrugged.

'Are you?'

He slipped the collar over Tango's head and tightened it a notch, then straightened. 'Not really. We've just walked all along the river wall, back along Rectory Road and down to the Quay for a look at the boats, then out on the river wall again to the woods. That was when she slid off. I ran after her, and then she caught sight of you and legged it. Not surprisingly, I couldn't keep up.'

He fell into step beside her, and she turned down off the river wall and headed back towards Rectory Road along another path across the marshes.

'So—why Butley Ford?' Maisie asked, telling herself it was just to make polite conversation, and nothing at all to do with her ravening curiosity.

James shrugged. 'I've always liked it. I used to come here on holiday when I was a boy, and stay with my grandfather. I needed a lifestyle change, and this house came up, and I thought, Why not? A job fell in my lap—it was just...'

'Meant?'

He laughed a little awkwardly. 'Sounds so stupid, but that's what it felt like.'

'I don't think it's stupid. Sometimes it just happens.'

He shot Maisie a curious glance. 'And you? Why did you end up here? How long have you been here?' he asked.

'Three years. There was a job, and my house was just sitting there needing a tenant, and—well, it just happened, really, rather like yours.'

He nodded. 'Like so much of life.'

'Do you believe in destiny?'

He laughed. 'No. I believe in careless coincidence and random happenings. Fate, if you like. I think we make our own destiny in how we pick our way through the hand fate throws us. What about you?'

She shrugged. 'I haven't really thought about it. How's the unpacking going?'

'Oh, don't,' he groaned. 'I must have been mad to move. It's a nightmare.' They came to a halt by his back gate, and he looked down into Maisie's eyes and nearly took the legs out from under her with his wry smile. 'I seem to have most of a jug of lemonade in my fridge, and a whole heap of biscuits. Fancy sharing?'

She did—quite desperately—but she had the dogs and cats to feed and the chickens to do, and she'd promised Anna she'd pop over and check on the pony's breathing.

'Another time,' she said, and to her disappointment he seemed to withdraw.

'Of course. I could do with straightening a few things up before I call it a day anyway.'

He opened the gate and went through it with

Tango, lifting his hand in farewell before closing it and shutting her out behind the solid wall of wood.

Curious how lonely that made her feel but, short of banging on the gate and telling him she'd changed her mind, there was nothing she could do.

Maisie shrugged. Kirsten would never have wasted such a golden opportunity, she told herself, but, then, she wasn't Kirsten. With a little shrug, she trudged along the lane outside the high brick wall that enclosed his garden, round the corner into Doctor's Lane and down to the Lodge.

There would be other opportunities to see him. She could wait.

CHAPTER TWO

ANY hope Maisie might have been cherishing about bumping into James again over the next couple of days was soon crushed.

It was one of those nightmare weekends when she wished she'd been a landscape gardener or a window cleaner or a filing clerk. Anything rather than a vet, working alone and wondering every time she sat down or tried to catch a nap how long it would be before the phone rang again and there was yet another emergency.

Not long enough, was the usual answer.

The surgery on Saturday morning was straightforward enough, apart from the dog with a foreign body in his ear. He had to be admitted for emergency surgery to remove it as soon as her consults were finished. The rest were mostly routine, including two cats for inoculation because the owner was off on holiday that day and had forgotten until they were about to go that the vaccination certificates had to be up to date before the cattery would accept them.

Easy mistake to make, Maisie thought, but there was really no excuse because the surgery sent out reminders. She signed the cards, sent them off on their holiday with a gently worded slap on the wrist and went out into the back.

'All ready when you are,' Kathy, the head nurse, told her.

'I need a cup of tea,' Maisie wailed, and found a mug in her hand.

'How did I know you'd say that?' Kathy teased.

'Creature of habit. You're a darling. How's the dog?'

'Morgan? He's fine. He keeps shaking his head and scratching, but I've put a lampshade on him so he can't get to it. He's just whimpering and looking mournful.'

Maisie laughed. The little cross-breed was a charmer, and she couldn't leave him suffering any longer. She swallowed her tea hastily and put the mug down.

'Come on, then, let's sedate him and get this seed out. At least, I hope that's what it is. I'm pretty sure, but he wouldn't really let me get a look.'

'It's that time of year—bit early, but it's been a mild spring.'

'And it's working up to being a hot summer,' Maisie said with feeling. She hated the heat, and to-day it was getting to her. Ever since she'd had that bug, she'd been hot and cold all over the place. Today she'd just been hot, and she knew it was going to be one of those weekends.

She injected a small amount of sedative into the vein in Morgan's leg while Kathy held him firmly. 'Hope that's enough. I don't want to give him too much, I want to send him home with his owners in a couple of hours. We don't need anything else to ba-bysit for the weekend.' As they watched, Morgan's eyes drooped and he keeled over, still semi-conscious but hopefully sufficiently unaware that she could pull out the foreign body without upsetting him.

She checked his heart again, made sure he was OK and then lifted up his ear flap and peered inside.

'Oh, yes, it's definitely a grass seed. Is he OK?'

Kathy nodded. 'Seems fine.'

'Right, hold him firmly, just in case he's not under enough,' she warned, and then with the long-nosed forceps she grasped the grass seed and pulled it out. He didn't even flinch, to her relief, and she examined the seed carefully to make sure it was intact.

'Right, that looks OK. It doesn't smell yet, so it can't have been in there long,' she said. The phone rang and as they were alone now in the surgery, Kathy answered it while Maisie carried on working. She listened for a moment, then cocked her head on one side and looked at Maisie.

'There's a horse with colic out at Earl Soham.'

There would be, she thought. It was miles.

'OK. Take all the details and tell them I'm on my way.' By the time Kathy had finished jotting down notes, Maisie was stripping off her gloves. 'Right, I've cleaned the ear out and given him a jab of antibiotic and reversed the sedation, so if you could finish off here for me and keep an eye on him—what else have we got in over the weekend?'

'Nothing much,' Kathy told her. 'The little cat on fluids, the hedgehog that was brought in yesterday—that's all.'

'Right. If you could make sure they're all OK before you go, I'll leave Morgan here in your capable hands. Thanks, Kathy, you're a star.'

She checked the boot of her car for everything she might need for this next emergency, and then as an afterthought popped back in and used the loo. The tea seemed to have gone straight through her, and goodness knows when she'd get another chance.

She left for her colicky horse, wondering what she'd find. It could vary between a bit of mild tummyache from overeating to a massive impaction of the bowel contents or a twisted gut, both the last potentially fatal and requiring urgent referral to Newmarket for surgery—or, if the owner was unable or unwilling to pay for surgery, euthanasia.

In the end it was a fairly straightforward colic. The mare was sweating up and pacing restlessly, biting at her sides and unable to stand still, but she wasn't throwing herself on the ground or trying to roll, which was always a good sign.

Maisie passed a tube up the mare's nose and down her throat, and checked it was in her stomach and not her lungs by sucking on the pipe. If it didn't smell foul, it wasn't the stomach. Simple test, really, but it turned her own stomach every time and today was no exception.

Luckily—or unfortunately, depending on whose side you were on—she'd got it right first time, and all she had to do now was mix a litre or so of liquid paraffin and hot water, shake them up together to try and make an emulsion and then hold the ghastly mixture aloft until it had drained down the pipe, something it was always curiously reluctant to do.

'OK, little lady,' she said soothingly, as the horse stamped her foot and moved restlessly around the box. 'Just a little longer.'

Her owner snorted. 'They should tell you at vet school that oil and water don't mix,' he said sagely as she struggled to hold the funnel in the air and keep moving with the horse.

'I tell you what, I'll swap,' Maisie said. 'You hold this, I'll hold the horse. Your height might help. I can never do this bit.'

'You need wellies with stilts on,' he teased, but he took over, to her relief, and with his extra height the paraffin mixture seemed to give up its struggle and slid obligingly down the tube into the horse's stomach.

She'd given the little mare an antispasmolytic and a sedative already, and it seemed to be working. They watched her for half an hour, and finally Maisie was happy that she was improving slowly. The horse was less restless, and with instructions to the owner to watch her constantly and report back in a couple of hours or immediately if there was any change for the worse, she stripped off her overalls, packed up her equipment and went back to her car.

The first thing she did was check her mobile phone for messages, and of course there were some.

Three, in fact—all in different directions, and none of them anywhere near a loo, she thought as she bounced down the farm track to the road. Still, at least they were nearer home. She stopped at the gate and rang the callers, wondering if any of them could get to the surgery. At least it had plumbing, and she could kill three birds with one stone and reunite Morgan with his owners at the same time.

She was in luck. Two she could advise over the phone, and the third was able to come in to the surgery, so she headed straight there. It was the last thing she wanted to do. She ached from end to end, she'd

got cramp in her arm from holding the funnel aloft
and trying to hold the restless mare's head reasonably
still, and if the nagging from her bladder was to be
believed, she probably had a urinary infection.

Great. Still, at least she was headed for the surgery
and not the middle of a field, she thought, and wondered if the rest of the weekend was going to be gov-
erned by her proximity to plumbing.

Oh, joy.

Sunday was no better, and by the end of Monday
morning she was considering a career change. Either
that or a week in bed. She came home for lunch, and
while she was outside, doing the chickens and playing
with the dogs, she could hear Tango barking. Funny.
She'd been barking that morning when she'd left for
work, but she'd assumed it had been because of the
postman.

She went back for her afternoon surgery, leaving
her dogs safely and happily enclosed in their outside
run with their toys and plenty of water, but when she
got back, Tango was still at it.

Not just once or twice, as if someone had rung the
doorbell, but the sad, continuous barking of a dog left
alone for hours.

James must have started his job, she thought, and
she felt anger rising in her. He shouldn't have got a
young dog if he didn't intend to give her time, and
Tango was obviously unhappy.

She took her dogs for a walk, wishing she could
take the young retriever too, and when she came back
the barking had stopped.

Good. Finally, he must be home.

She would have gone up his drive and said something to him, but yet again her bladder was nagging, and so she went straight home. Thank goodness she'd phoned the surgery earlier and made an appointment to see the doctor tomorrow, because this was getting worse and worse, and there seemed to be pressure on it rather than irritation.

From a mass of some sort?

No. She wouldn't let herself think about it, but at the back of her mind was the subconscious fear. She'd lost her mother to cancer when she'd been only twelve, and then her father two years ago, just before she'd moved here, but there was nothing to connect her to either of them, because she'd been adopted.

Nevertheless, the fear was there. The Big C. She saw enough of it at work, after all.

No! She wouldn't think about it. She'd discuss it with Dr Shearer tomorrow. It was probably nothing more or less than a simple urinary tract infection.

And what about the mass?

No. She was imagining it. There was no mass. It was probably just because she was due for a period.

She cooked herself a meal, then debated going next door to talk to James about leaving Tango, but she was just too tired. She'd talk to him when she saw him. She'd need plenty of energy for that particular confrontation...

How did he know he was in trouble?

There was just something about the purposeful stride of that diminutive little woman that made his heart sink.

Only his heart, though. Everything else was rising.

His blood pressure, his interest, his— Damn. He didn't need to be that interested in his neighbour!

James stopped walking and let her come to him, and when she was just close enough that he could have reached out and touched that feisty little chin with his fingers, she came to a halt.

'About Tango,' she began.

'Good morning. Beautiful day.'

'She barks when you're out.'

'I know.'

'She's frightened.'

'And you'd know this.'

'Yes, I'd know this. I'm a vet.'

'Ah.' He tipped his head on one side and studied her. 'You don't look old enough—'

'Don't change the subject! You shouldn't be leaving her all day—you were gone yesterday before I left in the morning, and you didn't get back until after me last night—and I'd been home for lunch, so I know you weren't there then, and she was barking the whole time! You can't simply leave a dog for eleven and a half hours, it's criminal!'

He opened his mouth to correct her, then shut it again. He couldn't be bothered to argue. She'd already tried and sentenced him in one fell swoop without giving him a chance to put his case, and, anyway, he was tired. He'd been woken up at some ungodly hour for the last four mornings, and he'd had enough. To hell with neighbourly relations.

'I tell you what,' he said tightly, 'I'll shut my dog up if you'll shut your cockerel up.'

'It's not my cockerel,' she snapped.

'Well, it's not my dog,' he snapped back. 'And,

anyway, my personal domestic arrangements are none of your damned business, so I'll thank you to butt out—and while you're at it, you could return the cockerel to the rightful owner so we can all get a bit of sleep.'

'Not easy. She's dead.'

'Lucky her,' he muttered. He shut his mouth with a snap and walked off.

At least, he would have done, but Tango and the two scruffy mutts at Maisie's feet were inextricably intertwined, and so his dignified exit on the moral high ground was reduced to farce as he struggled to separate the dogs without any help from the infernally irritating woman standing in front of him.

'You could do something useful,' he snarled, and one of her naturally pretty eyebrows lifted in an eloquent curve as she looked down on him.

She unclipped her dogs, removed their leads from the tangled mess and turned on her heel, the dogs falling into step behind her without a word from their mistress as she stalked off in dignified silence.

Damn.

And she still had the sexiest bottom he'd ever seen...

She was late, of course, because a rabbit had kindly presented with an explosively full abscess that had ruptured all over her as she'd palpated it and covered her with about a gallon of foul-smelling goo. She'd had to go home to wash, and yet again she'd heard Tango barking.

So much for her lecture! Still, she didn't have time to worry. She drove the short distance to save time,

and then, of course, she couldn't park the car. By the
time she had, it was six thirty-five and she would have
been quicker if she'd walked from home. She leant
on the counter, trying to get her breath because, of
course, she'd run from the side street where she'd
eventually abandoned the wretched vehicle. 'Maisie
McDowell,' she gasped. 'I've got an appointment
with Dr Shearer at six-thirty.'

The receptionist looked down at her computer
screen, then back up at Maisie with a frown. 'Six-
twenty, actually. I'm sorry, Miss McDowell, Dr
Shearer's left.'

'Left?'

'Well, you are fifteen minutes late.'

She dredged up a smile. 'I'm sorry. I had to go
home and change after work.'

The receptionist gave her a speaking look. 'I'm
sure Dr Shearer would rather have seen you on time
than not at all.'

'I doubt it,' Maisie muttered, and started to turn
away, but the thought of waiting any longer was too
much for her. She needed answers, and she needed
them tonight. She turned back. 'I don't suppose
there's another doctor still working? I really, really
need to see someone tonight,' she said, and she was
conscious of a tremor in her voice.

Perhaps the woman heard it too, because she un-
bent a little, albeit unwillingly. 'Well, Dr Sutherland's
still here, but he's been very busy and he has just
finished. I'll buzz him and see if he'll see you, but I
wouldn't hold out much hope.'

'Dr Sutherland?' Maisie said, puzzled. She'd never
heard of a Dr Sutherland, but the receptionist was

ignoring her, talking on the phone, and she looked up and gave Maisie a chilly smile.

'You're lucky. He says he'll see you if it's that urgent, just go straight in.'

'Thank you.'

Maisie turned and headed for the consulting rooms. Damn. She didn't mind seeing a male doctor really, but she had hoped to see Jane Shearer, just because being prodded about in that area was something she'd rather have done by a woman doctor, given a choice.

Still, better this Dr Sutherland than waiting any longer, she thought, and knocked on the door.

At the peremptory 'Come in!' she opened it, stepped inside and came to a grinding halt.

'Maisie?'

Of all people. He closed his eyes and counted to ten, then dragged in a good, deep breath and looked up into those startled toffee-coloured eyes. The last time he'd seen them they'd been spitting amber sparks, and absolutely the last thing he needed was another conversation with the neighbour from hell.

'I didn't know you were a doctor,' she said accusingly, and he gave an inward sigh.

'You didn't ask,' he pointed out fairly, but she wasn't in the mood to be fair, obviously.

'I thought you were working in London.'

'London?' He was astonished and perhaps a touch irritated, and he wondered if it came over in his voice. He decided he didn't much care. 'Why would I live here and commute to London?'

She shrugged. 'People do. Kirsten thought—'

'Ah. The lovely Kirsten. Kirsten seems to think I

want to have my house professionally co-ordinated—
by her, of course.' He swung his chair round and met
her eyes candidly. 'Presumably because I'm a fat cat
from the city.'

She had the grace to blush. 'I think it was the antiques,' she said, trying to explain and failing.

His mouth twitched. 'Ah, yes. The millstones.
Family heirlooms, actually. I'm sort of stuck with
them—a caretaker for future generations of little
Sutherlands, God help them. Anyway, now you're
here, and now you know I'm a doctor, which is presumably why you're here, why don't you sit down
and tell me the reason for your visit?'

It was obviously the last thing in the world she
wanted to do, but after an inward battle she sat,
looked him in the eyes and said candidly, 'There's
something pressing on my bladder. Some kind of
mass.' She hesitated. 'I think it could be cancer.'

He settled back in his chair, hands steepled under
his chin, and eyed her curiously.

'Cancer?'

She nodded, and he wondered what on earth made
her think it was cancer. Although, as she was a vet...

'Tell me your symptoms, from the beginning. What
was the first thing you noticed?'

She blinked and stared at him for a moment.
'Um...oh, well, I suppose feeling ill. I thought it was
a bug, but now I'm beginning to wonder. I felt dreadful for a few weeks, and I'm still not right. Some
things taste odd.'

'Odd?'

Maisie shrugged. 'I can't really explain. I just seem

fussier than I was. And then a week or so ago I started
needing to pee very often—'

'Any pain or unusual odour?'

Dear God. He was talking about her bladder to the
neighbour from hell, and judging by the look on her
face she was not impressed!

'No,' she said. 'No pain, no odour.'

He moved on, wondering how this question would
land. 'Bowels OK?'

She squirmed uncomfortably under his scrutiny,
and despite her rising colour didn't allow her eyes to
drop from his. 'Fine,' she said shortly.

'How about your periods? Regular? Lighter or
heavier than usual, or any discomfort on intercourse?'

She sucked in her breath, and he found himself
holding his. He really, really didn't want to know
about her sex life.

'I don't have a regular cycle,' she told him. 'I must
have a period due at any time, though.'

He noticed that she'd ignored the part about intercourse when she'd answered his question. Was that
deliberate? 'So when was your last period?' he asked,
dealing with that first.

She felt her brow crease in thought. 'I have no
idea.'

'Before the onset of these symptoms?'

She nodded slowly. 'Probably. I had one during the
snow—that would have been the first week in
February.'

'You seem very certain of that.'

She looked acutely uncomfortable. 'I am. We had
snow, I couldn't get out to go to the shops. I...um...'

She trailed off, and the penny dropped. He suppressed a smile. 'Right. And nothing since?'

She shook her head, puzzlement showing on her face. 'I don't think so.'

Good grief. It was now the beginning of June! Surely she was more aware of her cycle than that? Hardly anybody was *that* irregular. Unless...

'Just hop up on the couch and let me have a look at you,' he said, and she undid her jeans and he slid his hands under the edge of the denim and probed and prodded her abdomen. She avoided his eyes, staring fixedly at the wall, and just to be certain he was very thorough. He could feel her heart pounding, though, and the fear he could sense in her was climbing higher with every passing second.

'Any pain?'

She shook her head and squirmed as he pressed down just under the rim of her pubic bone. 'Just pressure.'

Lord, it was so obvious. How had she not noticed? 'What about clothes—everything still fit you?'

She frowned at him. 'Clothes? Of course they still fit—well, except for the fact that I've gained weight. I haven't started losing it yet, if that's what you're getting at.'

He turned away to hide his smile. 'Not at all. Quite the opposite. You can get down from there now, I'm pretty sure I know what's wrong.'

'And?' she said, sliding off the couch and fastening her jeans with trembling fingers. She had one foot half in, half out of her trainers when he sat down again and studied her thoughtfully.

'Well, you're right, of course, there is a mass in

your abdomen, but it's nothing to worry about. At least, it's not going to kill you, and it's a self-limiting condition.'

'So you think it's an abscess?' she said, and he could see the relief in her eyes. 'Thank God for that. I'd managed to convince myself...' She sat down, wriggling her foot into her shoe and tugging up the laces with one hand while she smiled at him in relief.

'No, I don't think it's an abscess,' he said, returning her smile wryly. 'But I estimate that it will have resolved itself in about four to six months—well, all bar the next eighteen years, or so. That could be a little more tricky.'

'Eighteen...? What on earth are you talking about?'

He arched a brow. 'Call yourself a vet, Maisie?' he said softly. 'I should have thought it was obvious. You're pregnant.'

The blood drained from her face, and for a second he thought she was going to pass out. Then her colour returned, and she sat up slowly and stared at him, her shoe forgotten.

'Don't be ridiculous! I can't possibly be pregnant.'

'They all say that, but unfortunately no method of contraception is infallible.'

'Mine is,' she said tightly.

'Apparently not. Just because you don't want to admit it, that won't change the facts. I'm sorry, Maisie, you may not like it but you're going to have a baby. I'd stake my career on it.'

She got to her feet, and gathered herself up to her full five feet four. 'Good,' she said clearly. 'It may come to that, because there's no way on God's earth

I can be pregnant, *Dr* Sutherland, because I haven't been in a relationship for over two years, and not even elephants are pregnant that long!'

'Nevertheless—'

She cut him off, the bit between her teeth and determined to have her say. 'I *know* I can't be pregnant,' she said emphatically, 'and if that's the only thing you're prepared to consider, then you deserve to be struck off for incompetence, and I shall do my best to make sure it happens! I knew GPs were hard to come by these days, but I didn't realise they were scraping quite *that* far down into the bottom of the barrel!'

And wrenching the door open, she stalked out.

James sat back in his chair and winced. Ouch. The bottom of the barrel, eh? Nice one, Sutherland. Very well handled.

Oh, well, she'd get over it. She'd remember her one-night stand eventually, and come crawling back for antenatal care.

Or a termination.

He didn't want to think about that one, but it was Maisie's problem, not his, and he had no intention of provoking any further discussion with her on the subject. She could see someone else next time, he'd had it with going head to head with a woman whose tongue could lash the skin off you at fifty paces.

Let her deal with it herself.

He packed up his desk, shut down his computer and picked up his bag.

No. He wouldn't feel guilty. It was hardly his fault she couldn't remember having had sex. She'd only remembered her last period because she'd obviously had a supplies crisis when she'd been cut off by the snow. Not much of a boy scout, our Maisie, he thought wryly. Anyway, she should be grateful to him for putting her mind at rest. Pregnancy, even unplanned and evidently unexpected, was a damned sight better than cancer.

He headed for home, his conscience clear.

Sort of.

Maisie slammed the consulting-room door behind her—or she would have done, but the door-closer resisted her efforts and all she got for her sins was a tearing pain in her wrist and a broken nail.

Damn. Damn, damn and double damn.

Tears blurring her vision, she ran out into the street, one foot still half in, half out of her shoe, found her car more by luck than judgement and drove blindly home, her wrist still stabbing with pain.

He was crazy. There was no way she was pregnant, she thought, sitting in the car on her drive and still seething with anger, and only one way to prove it to him. She'd go and buy a pregnancy test.

She backed out into the lane, scrubbing the tears from her cheeks, and drove one-handed to the supermarket in a nearby town.

Twenty minutes later she arrived home, went into the bathroom armed with the test and the instructions and set out to prove him wrong.

CHAPTER THREE

SHE wasn't at home.

James stood at her front door, eyeing her car thoughtfully and listening for the dogs, but they were silent. He pressed the doorbell again and heard it echo, as doorbells always seemed to in an empty house.

She wasn't there. And somehow he just knew where she'd be.

Ignoring Tango and his guilt, because he had enough guilt about Maisie to sink a battleship and Tango, bless her heart, would survive a little further neglect, he headed down the path across the marshes and up onto the river wall, and there in the distance was a small hump.

As he walked towards it, his guilt prodding at him, the hump resolved itself into a person seated on the edge of the path. Another minute and he could see it was her, and the dogs were with her. They turned their heads towards him, watching him intently, but she didn't so much as glance his way.

He didn't fancy his reception, but he couldn't leave her here and ignore her—not after the way he'd broken the news to her. He'd been hugely unprofessional, because he was nothing like detached enough, and once he'd got over his self-righteous fit and had had time to think about it, he'd been disgusted with himself.

Disgusted, and worried about her.

And anyway, what if he *was* wrong? If, as she'd said, she hadn't had a relationship with a man for two years, then there was no way she could be pregnant.

Unless the unthinkable had happened.

No. Don't be melodramatic, he told himself. She's just shocked because some one-night stand she's almost forgotten about has had repercussions.

The thought of her having a one-night stand brought bile to his throat, but he swallowed it and carried on walking slowly towards her, stopping only when he was a mere stride away.

She didn't look up, but the dogs wagged their tails, to his relief. He didn't fancy being eaten by them, and he didn't put it past Maisie to have trained them to attack.

He lowered himself to the path beside her and sat staring out over the river. She still didn't acknowledge his presence but, then again, she didn't get up and walk away either, and he hadn't really expected her to greet him with open arms.

'I owe you an apology,' he said softly. 'I handled that consultation with all the skill and tact of a bulldozer.'

'You were right.'

'Pardon?'

'You were right. I am pregnant. I bought a test.'

He turned his head and studied her, and saw the lines of strain etched on her face. Tears had dried on her cheeks, the moisture stripped out of them by the sun and the wind, and the salt trails ran down to her chin. His heart went out to her.

'Maisie, I'm really sorry. I don't know what to say.'

'You could tell me how,' she said, her voice stunned with disbelief. He stared at her, the flippant reply hovering on the tip of his tongue, but the utter bewilderment on her face stopped it in its tracks. She looked shocked to the core, and James realised that he was dealing with something very much more complex here than simple denial, something that was going to take all his skill and understanding to help her through.

Maisie really didn't seem to have any idea how she could have become pregnant.

And that left only one—highly unpalatable—answer.

She felt his hand under her elbow, and realised he'd stood up. 'Come on. I'm going to take you home and make you something to eat and drink.'

'I don't want anything—'

'Tough. Come on.'

His voice was gentle but implacable, and she let him lift her to her feet and lead her home.

His home, not hers, she noticed vaguely as they turned up his drive.

'I need to feed the cats.'

'Later. They'll manage a bit longer.'

He led her in through the scullery with its wonderful sink, and Tango greeted them rapturously.

'Hello, silly dog,' she said gently, rubbing the dog's head quite automatically when she found it almost in her face. 'Get down.'

She got down, but probably because James had

hauled her off and sent her out into the enclosed rear garden with the other two to let off steam together. Of course, Jodie and Scamp knew exactly where they were, and rushed off to smell all the new and exciting smells.

How wonderful to have such simple things to worry about, when she—

'How?' she said to herself for the hundredth time, but James must have heard, because he took her elbow again and led her through into the kitchen and pushed her gently into one of the sofas.

'I don't know. We'll talk it through. Let me make some tea.'

'I don't want tea. I just want answers.'

'You need both.'

He filled the kettle, and she watched him absently and wondered why he was bothering to be nice to her when she'd been so rude to him that morning.

Even if he had deserved it.

And she'd been rude to him this evening as well. Oh, lord.

'Look, I'm really sorry about today. I shouldn't have said what I did about scraping the bottom of the barrel.'

His mouth quirked. 'I've heard worse things, and I have to say this time I had it coming,' he said gently. Then he was pushing a mug of tea into her hands and sitting down beside her, one arm resting on the back and his body turned so he was facing her. He hitched a knee up onto the cushion, his foot tucked behind the other leg, and settled back, studying her with those extraordinary ice-blue eyes.

'Do you believe in virgin births?' she asked sud-

denly before he could speak, and he smiled, a rueful,
regretful smile, and shook his head.

'No, I don't.'

'So—how, James? How on earth have I got pregnant? I mean, it's not like I get drunk and sleep
around—I couldn't live a more blameless existence.'

'Nobody's trying to blame you, Maisie. Let's get
that clear right from the start.' He paused for a moment, his lips pursed, then met her eyes. 'Your last
period.'

'Back to that again?'

'You're sure it was in January or February?'

She nodded. 'Yes, quite sure. I can even tell you the
day. It was a Sunday—the first Sunday in February.'

'OK. Well, from examining you I would say you're
about somewhere between fifteen and twenty weeks
pregnant. If we take that first Sunday in February as
day one, that makes you about seventeen weeks pregnant, according to my ready reckoner, which is spot
on for how you felt. I'd say your baby's due in early
November.'

She stared at him numbly. It all seemed so unreal.
How could she be having a baby? She couldn't look
after a baby and go to work. And anyway, there was
still the insurmountable problem of how it had been
conceived. There was no way—

'Now, I want you to think back. You say your cycle's irregular, so working forwards from that last period, can you think of any time in the following few
weeks when you woke up in the morning and didn't
remember going to bed? Maybe if you'd been out, or
away...'

'I don't go out, not like that, and I haven't been away—'

She broke off, a sudden, shocking thought occurring to her. It must have shown in her face, because James removed the mug gently from her trembling fingers and set it down, then took her hands in his. His grip was warm and reassuring, an anchor in a suddenly wild sea.

'What, Maisie? What have you remembered? Tell me.'

She shook her head. 'I can't tell you. I don't know,' she said, and her voice sounded strange and far-away. 'I don't remember anything—well, nothing significant, really.'

'Try,' he urged.

So she tried, scraping about in her patchy memory for as much information as she could muster.

'I was at a conference—an equine anaesthetics symposium in Newmarket. One of my old lecturers was there, too—a clinical pharmacology professor. I hadn't seen him for years. He was alone, and we were drinking in the bar. He was telling me all about his wife leaving him.'

She shook her head to clear it. 'I felt sorry for him. He'd had a car accident, and he said things had gone wrong from then onwards. We had quite a few drinks, I suppose, and I woke up in the morning feeling really rough and wondering why I'd let him get me so drunk. It never occurred to me, not even when I saw it in the paper, but— Oh, God.'

She felt his hands tighten on hers reassuringly. 'What did you see in the paper?'

'He hanged himself,' she said slowly. 'In police

custody. He'd been arrested for putting something in a girl's drink—the barman had seen him and called the police, and they'd arrested him. It was a couple of weeks after the conference, and I was really shocked. I remember telling Kirsten, laughing about it a bit hysterically, saying I'd had a lucky escape— but I hadn't, had I? I hadn't escaped at all, I just hadn't remembered.'

She turned blindly to him, locking onto his eyes for confirmation of what she already knew.

'Oh, my God. He must have put something in my drink, and then...'

James nodded, his eyes full of compassion and something else that she didn't quite understand. She felt her eyes fill with tears, and as the first one slid down her cheek, she felt his arms come round her and wrap her safely against the hard, solid warmth of his chest.

James wanted to kill someone.

The bastard who had done this to her would be a good start, but he was already dead. Probably a good thing. Murder didn't sit well with the Hippocratic oath.

Her hands tightened convulsively on his shirt and he heard her gulp on the sobs that were fighting their way out of her body.

'Do I have to tell the police?' she asked, her voice filled with dread, and he forced himself to breathe nice and deep and steady, and rubbed a hand gently over her back.

'Not if you don't want to,' he said, not sure if it was true but sure that, for now at least, it was what

Maisie needed to hear. 'What would it achieve? He's dead, Maisie. You can't press charges against a dead person. The only person this affects is you. If you want to go to the police, then I'll support you, but I don't think there's any point. I think you should concentrate your energies on dealing with the here and now.'

She stayed rigid for a minute more, then he felt the sobs rising in her again and she collapsed against his chest. He shifted, easing her closer, and somehow she ended up on his lap, burrowing into his shoulder, her body heaving.

He held her for what seemed like an age, until the sobs died away and she was still, then she pushed up and turned her head away.

'I'm sorry... I don't know why I— Oh, hell, I never cry.'

'I think you have a pretty good excuse.'

She sniffed, and he pulled a spare, clean handkerchief out of his pocket and put it in her hand.

'Thanks,' she mumbled. She blew her nose and scrubbed at her eyes, then looked at the handkerchief and laughed unsteadily. 'You're going to run out at this rate.'

'At least you'll know what to buy me for Christmas,' he teased, and she smiled, but then the smile faded and she shifted away from him, into the corner of the sofa.

James let her go, sensing that it was all part of the process of coming to terms with what had happened to her. For a moment she chewed her lip, then she looked up at him, then away again, as if she was struggling with her words.

Finally she spoke, her voice quiet and strained. 'I feel—is violated too strong a word?'

He crushed his anger. 'No. No, I don't think it is. I think I would feel the same.'

She shot him a surprised look. 'Really? I thought men didn't worry about that sort of thing. Sex at any price and so on. I would have thought the average man would simply be annoyed that he couldn't remember it.'

He gave a short, startled laugh. 'Well, I don't know about the average man, but that certainly doesn't apply to me. The idea of anyone drugging me so they could use my body for something so essentially private and personal would make me very deeply angry—but, then, I may be a bit of an oddball. I can't imagine wanting to get that close to a woman with whom I wasn't involved body and soul. I just don't do it. So, no, I don't think violated is too strong a word.'

A shudder ran through her, and she wriggled further away from him, hitching herself right up into the far corner of the sofa as if their conversation had brought it home to her that she was alone with him, and how vulnerable that made her. He wanted to reassure her, to tell her that she was safe with him, but he knew she wouldn't believe him yet, and possibly never after this, simply because he was a man.

Except that this man wanted nothing more than to hold her and protect her and cherish her...

Hell's teeth. Where had that come from?

He stood up abruptly, moving away from her to give both of them more space. 'Another cup of tea?'

She shook her head. 'I should go home.'

'Not until you've eaten.'

And there were things they needed to discuss, tests that needed to be run to make sure that she and the baby were safe, but now was not the time to introduce any other fears or to consider whether or not she was going to continue with the pregnancy. For now, she needed to know that there was one person in the world she could trust absolutely, and he intended to make damned sure she could.

And that meant that, for now at least, he'd have to put his own personal interest very firmly on hold.

Maisie knew what he was doing.

Slowly, reassuringly, he moved about the kitchen, throwing together something that smelt absolutely wonderful and keeping up a steady stream of meaningless conversation while she sipped her third cup of tea and the dogs lay in heaps around her feet. She'd behave the same way with a wary, injured animal, and the thought made her smile a little inside.

'I'm not going to fall apart,' she told him softly, and he paused for a moment, then shot her a crooked smile.

'I didn't think you were.'

'You're cosseting me.'

'Don't you think you deserve it?'

She laughed a little raggedly. 'Probably not. I was stupid, wasn't I? Putting myself in that position.'

'What—having a few drinks with someone you'd learned to respect? I wouldn't say you'd done anything wrong at all.'

'Except leave an unguarded drink.'

'Were you in a nightclub or drinking with strangers?'

The ragged laugh sounded again in her ears as she remembered the very sedate and civilised surroundings of the hotel bar. 'Hardly. We were in the hotel lounge.'

'I rest my case. Do you like ginger and garlic?'

'Love them.'

'Good, because it's just occurred to me I've put rather a lot in if you don't like it.'

'What about your patients?' she asked, and he just shrugged and grinned.

'I tell them all to eat lots of garlic because it protects the heart and is a wonderful natural antibiotic. The flip side is they hopefully don't notice if I smell of it.'

She chuckled, then her smile faded as the reality of her situation came crashing back. Oh, lord...

'Come on. It's ready.'

She looked up, to see two plates on the table heaped with a colourful extravaganza. Her stomach rumbled, and she got up and went over, deliberately shutting her mind to unwelcome thoughts. 'Looks good. Miss Keeble would be scandalised at you, though, eating in the kitchen,' she said with a weak attempt at a smile, and he chuckled.

'Miss Keeble would no doubt be scandalised at all sorts of things that I've done, but fortunately for me she isn't here to worry about it.'

'I think she would have liked you. You're a good cook—that would help. This is delicious.'

He smiled, his eyes softening, and she felt hugely guilty for the way she'd criticised him.

'I'm so sorry about the way I spoke to you,' she said, putting her fork down. She couldn't eat until she'd got this off her chest, but he just waved his own fork at her and shook his head.

'Don't worry. Eat.'

But there was something else troubling her, and she ploughed on. 'About Tango barking...'

'Tango hates being left alone. I'll come back before I go on my calls, if I can, and take her for a run, then after my calls I'll come home for lunch and take her out again, or play with her in the garden. Then she'll be alone again while I do my evening surgery and any other calls, but that's only a couple of hours, four at the most if I'm the duty doctor. Besides, it's only temporary and it's probably better than being in kennels. She's not mine, she's my sister's. When she comes back, Tango goes.'

And now she felt really bad.

'Stop it. Eat your food.'

He must have read her mind. Maisie had another forkful and tipped her head on one side, meeting his enquiring eyes. 'How about if she spent the day with Jodie and Scamp in the run in my garden? They get on well, and mine are so laid-back they'll help her settle. Then I wouldn't have to worry about her. I come home for lunch, too, after we finish operating, and I take them for a walk then. There's usually a lull until afternoon surgery, unless I've got a large animal call, so there's plenty of time.'

'Whatever. Eat, for goodness' sake, it'll be cold. We'll worry about Tango later, if you insist.'

'I do.'

He threw up his hands. 'Fine. Have her. Do what-

ever makes you happy. Now, eat, woman, for goodness' sake.'

She nodded, relieved that the dog, at least, was
sorted for now. Her own problems—well, she just
wouldn't think about them for a little while. There'd
be plenty of time later.

'Tell me about Miss Keeble,' he said suddenly.

She looked up and found him watching her again,
a thoughtful expression on his face.

'Miss Keeble? She was a treasure. Lonely—bit of
a funny old stick. Not everyone liked her, but she was
very good to me. We got on really well, and I did
what I could for her.'

'Did she have money? There was very little evidence of it being spent on the house in recent years,
but some people get a little eccentric in their later
years.'

Maisie laughed. 'No, she didn't have any money at
all. I don't think she'd ever owned her own home,
she'd gone from her parents' home straight into ser-
vice.'

His eyebrows shot up. 'So how did she end up with
this house? Was she a drug baron or something exciting?'

Maisie chuckled. 'Hardly. She was the doctor's
housekeeper. He used to live here in the Mount, and
the Lodge was his surgery. There's a gate in the
wall—'

'Yes, I've seen it. Perhaps we should get it working
again if I'm going to keep Tango in your garden with
your dogs. Save having to take her out on the road.'

'Good idea. Anyway, he retired, but Miss Keeble
carried on looking after him until he died, and he left

her both houses, in gratitude for services rendered. Rumour has it he was a cantankerous old man, but they looked after each other till the end, and she spoke very fondly of him.'

'And she had no money to maintain it all.'

'That's right. He only left her the houses, and she didn't have any money to keep them up. That's why she took in paying guests in the summer, and rented out the Lodge. When I moved here three years ago, she let it to me, and when she died, I found she'd left it to me in her will.'

'Good lord. None of my landlords have ever given me so much as a lightbulb, never mind a house!'

Maisie laughed. 'I know. The distant cousin who got this house queried it, but not as hard as I did. Believe me, nobody was more surprised than I was. I'm still waiting for someone to come along and tell me the will was dodgy and it's not mine. I have to pinch myself sometimes, but maybe she felt she'd been given it herself and she could do what she liked with it—and don't forget, I got the animals, too, so it wasn't quite the open-handed gesture it sounds like!'

'Animals?'

'Yes. Jodie and Scamp were hers, but there were also the cats—three of them, a ginger kitten and two elderly tabbies. Not that the kitten's a kitten any more. You're bound to have seen them. They haunt your garden.'

'Tango chases them.'

She chuckled. 'I'm sure. And then there were the chickens.'

'Ah.' James tipped his head on one side and gave her a wry smile. 'The cockerel with the dead owner.'

'Mmm. Hector.'

He snorted. 'Hector? How appropriate. I think it means bully, doesn't it?'

'He's glorious.'

'Not at four o'clock in the morning,' James said sternly, and if she hadn't seen the glimmer of humour in her eye, she would have thought the old cock's days were numbered.

'I could try shutting him in, but with these light mornings they get up early to enjoy the day...'

He made a rude noise and topped up her water glass, only the trickling sound breaking the sudden slightly tense silence.

She had a wonderful idea. 'Do you like eggs?'

He eyed her suspiciously, and she felt the smile tugging at her mouth as he set down the water jug. 'Going to bribe me? Or trying to kill me with cholesterol?'

She shook her head. 'Old wives' tale. They've changed their minds. Dietary cholesterol is almost insignificant compared to the amount made by our own bodies, and anyway it's saturated fat you need to cut down on. Eggs have good cholesterol and are very healthy.'

He chuckled. 'You're very convincing. I understood the jury was still out.'

She shrugged and smiled. 'Some sceptics like to hang onto the old myths...'

'Thank you. Eggs would be lovely. I eat about two a week.'

'But have you ever had a real egg? From a real, happy, free-range chicken?'

'Would they be the free-range chickens I found in

the borders the other day and had to chase out of the garden before they ate all the flowers?'

She felt her colour rise. Oh, dear, was there no end to the havoc she was causing in his life? 'I'm sorry. They still think they live here. I have to rescue them all the time.'

'Can't you clip their wings?'

'But the wall's so low at the side they can hop over it,' she explained. 'They'd need cannon-balls tied to their feet to stop them.'

'I'm sure it can be arranged,' he said drily, and she wasn't sure if he was joking. 'Although if we get the gate working, no doubt they'll just drag themselves through it, cannon-balls and all.'

'I'll do something about their run,' she promised. In fact, she'd been meaning to, because she was losing eggs and one of the chickens had disappeared, probably courtesy of Mr Fox.

'So, how about a cup of coffee and some of those delicious biscuits of yours to finish off?' he suggested, and she realised to her amazement that she'd eaten every scrap on her plate. How she'd found time to do that and talk so much she didn't know, but he'd successfully distracted her from the chaos her life had so recently descended into.

Not any more, though. Her hunger taken care of, reality had come crashing back with all the subtlety of an express train, and she pushed her plate away and shook her head.

'No. Really. That was lovely, but I couldn't eat another thing. I have to go back and feed the chickens and shut them up in their useless run, and I still haven't done the cats, and the dogs will be hungry—'

'I doubt it. They've had some of Tango's food—'

'Did you feed them?'

He smiled wryly. 'They seemed to think it was a good idea.'

'I'm sure.' She was debating pointing out that he shouldn't have fed them without consulting her, and then abandoned the idea. He'd been kindness itself, and without him she'd probably still be sitting on the river wall, contemplating throwing herself in or selling her story to a Sunday paper. She could see the headline now—VIRGIN VET IN PREGNANCY PUZZLE.

Well, hardly a virgin, but she might as well have been for all the difference it would have made.

'I still can't believe that such a respectable, decent person as Phillip Stevenson would have done that.'

'Phillip Stevenson?'

'My pharmacology professor—and, if the evidence is to be believed, the father of my baby.'

Baby. Dear God. She got up abruptly and walked out into the garden, suddenly feeling shut in. What had happened that night? Had she fought him? Passed out?

Enjoyed it?

She shuddered. Most unlikely. She'd respected him—well, until she'd seen the paper—and he'd always seemed a nice enough guy. Certainly clever, and reasonably good-looking when he'd been younger, she was sure. But she'd absolutely never seen him in anything other than his professional capacity as a lecturer when she'd been a student, and she certainly wouldn't have entertained a relationship with him—

'Penny for them.'

She sucked in a huge deep breath and let it out

with a whoosh. 'I was thinking about Phillip. He'd always seemed so decent. He said his marriage had fallen apart after the accident. I wonder if he had a head injury—if it changed him.'

'Possibly. It can certainly cause personality changes. Did he seem different?'

She nodded slowly, thinking back. 'Yes. More...I don't know. Intense, perhaps? I felt a little uncomfortable. I remember that.' She wrapped her arms around her body, hugging herself. 'I think I want to go home.'

'Sure. I'll walk you back.'

He locked the door with Tango on what she obviously considered to be the wrong side of it, and, gathering up the dogs, he shepherded them all home, pausing at her front door while she rummaged in her pocket for the keys. Finally she found them and opened the door, then hesitated.

'Thank you for everything,' she said quietly. 'I don't know what I would have done if you hadn't come and found me.'

'Don't thank me. I should have listened to you more closely, but I was still feeling mad about you telling me how to look after Tango.'

'I'm so sorry about that.'

He laid his finger on her lips, cutting off the words. 'No. Forget it. It's all past.' His eyes were troubled, searching her face, and she felt curiously naked. 'Will you be OK on your own?'

She nodded. 'I feel safe in my house. I've got the dogs.'

'I thought they lived outside?'

Her laugh sounded strained, even to her ears. 'Only

when I'm at work. At night they sleep outside my bedroom—unless I forget to close the door properly, and then they sneak onto the bed in the night and I find them there in the morning. I think tonight I might forget to close the door.'

His chuckle was warm and gentle, his breath puffing against her cheek. He was standing close to her, but she didn't feel threatened. Odd, that. She would have thought she might have done, under the circumstances, but she seemed to know instinctively that she was safe with James.

She turned to push the door open, and gasped as pain stabbed through her wrist.

'What is it?'

'Nothing. My wrist twinged—I hurt it earlier.'

Not for the life of her could she tell him that she'd strained it trying to slam the door of his consulting room, but then he took her hand in his, turning it over, carefully flexing it, his fingers probing. It might have hurt. She had no idea. All she was aware of was the warmth of his hands around hers, the firm yet gentle touch that made her want to cry.

'Put some ice on it now and before you go to bed, and put a support bandage on it before you do anything. If it's still sore in the morning let me know. I can let you have some anti-inflammatory gel to put on it if you need it. I don't want you to take anything like ibuprofen—not with the baby.'

Baby. Oh lord.

'I've got arnica and witch-hazel gel—I'll use that,' she said, and gave him what felt like a very brittle smile. 'Thanks again. I'll see you in the morning with Tango, shall I?'

'Sure. About half-seven?'

'OK.'

He lifted a hand in farewell and turned, walking the few steps to the lane and then turning the corner out of sight.

She closed the door slowly and sagged against it.

Baby. My God, she thought, and her hand slid down and cradled it. I'm going to have a baby.

CHAPTER FOUR

IT WAS a strange night.

Maisie couldn't sleep, probably not surprisingly, and she gave up in the end and curled up on the window-seat in her bedroom, the dogs at her side, staring out over the eerie silver landscape.

She could see the moon's reflection on the river as it snaked through the marshes, and beyond it in the distance, at the north end of Orford Ness, on the spit of land that separated Orford and Butley Ford from the sea, was the lighthouse, winking its warning every few seconds as the beam swept across the horizon.

It was peaceful, and she sat there with the window open and listened to the quiet rustlings and occasional cries that broke the silence.

And as she sat, contemplating the moonlit marshes, peace seemed to steal over her, calming her anger and soothing her fears, so that all she could think about was the baby growing within her, the innocent life that Phillip's actions had inadvertently created.

No. She wouldn't dwell on that. She wasn't ready to think about him yet, so she shut out any thought of the man who'd done this to her, and concentrated instead on the knowledge that in a few more months she'd be a mother.

How amazing. And she'd be a good one, not like her own mother, who'd abandoned her, given her up for adoption when she'd been just hours old and

walked away without a backward glance. When she'd
turned eighteen and had tried to contact her birth
mother, the woman hadn't been interested, and Maisie
could still remember vividly the pain of that rejection
as her dreams of a loving reconciliation had crumbled
into dust.

Deprived of the possibility of a relationship with
the woman who'd given her life, she'd clung to mem-
ories of her *real* mother, the woman who'd opened
her heart and her home to another woman's child, and
who'd been the most loving and caring and understanding person she'd ever met. Losing her to cancer
had been devastating to Maisie, but she'd never forgotten the warmth and generosity of her love, and she
vowed that her own baby, too, would know that same
unconditional love.

And thanks to Miss Keeble, bless her heart, at least
she had a home to offer her child, a home that she
owned free and clear. If she was careful, she could
possibly cope on a part-time salary. It would be tight,
but she'd manage.

'We'll be all right, baby,' she said softly, her hand
creeping down to cover the tiny bulge that was her
child. 'We'll be all right.'

The quiet night was giving way to dawn, and down
in the garden she heard Hector's early morning call.
She sighed. So late already? If she was going to get
any work done today, she ought to try and catch a
couple of hours' sleep, at least.

As she stood up stiffly, stretching to ease out the
kinks induced by sitting there for hours, she glanced
across at James's house. Which was his bedroom?
She'd thought it was the one on the front corner, the

one she could see from her room, but in the few days since he'd moved in the lights had been on in so many of the rooms when she'd gone to bed each night that she'd never managed to work it out.

Now, though, she could see that the windows of that corner bedroom, with the lovely views over both the river and the town, were open, and as she stood there, she saw a shape move inside the room, backlit by the moonlight from the other window.

The sash slid shut with a little thump, and she suppressed a guilty smile.

Oops. Hector had got him up again. She stood motionless, watching the window for any further sign of movement, then after an age a dark shape detached itself from the glass and moved away, silhouetted again by the moonlight flooding through the room.

Seeing him there was curiously comforting—reassuring, somehow. She felt less isolated, less alone in the world, knowing he was there. Ridiculous, really. He was only a neighbour, another GP in the practice she was registered with. Nothing more. She'd only seen him in his professional capacity by accident, and yet they'd argued about Tango and Hector, and he'd taken her into his home, fed her, cared for her, talked to her patiently and sympathetically through the most difficult moment of her adult life.

Why? No doubt he was asking himself that at that very moment, wondering what on earth he'd done to deserve her. Probably still feeling guilty about his less-than-sympathetic consultation, but to be fair there was no way he could have told her that would have made any difference.

Poor James. She'd keep out of his way for a while, try and cut him a bit of slack.

Starting by shutting Hector up at night.

'Bloody chicken!'

James stood at the window, glowering down into Maisie's garden and contemplating murder.

He'd had little enough sleep as it was, with Maisie's problems milling round and round in his head, and now that dratted bird had started with the crowing. If he had any sense at all he'd move into another bedroom. There was a wonderful one at the other end of the house, the mirror image of this one, with the same stunning views out over the marshes to the front but over the woodland at the side instead of towards the town.

And Maisie.

He glanced at her house, and for a moment he thought he saw her there at the window, her face ghostly pale in the moonlight.

No. He'd imagined it, poor, sad old fool that he was. He went back to bed, chastising himself soundly for fantasising about her in her bedroom, and spent the next two hours wide awake thinking about nothing else, while Hector went almost unnoticed.

'Good morning.'

She smiled up at him, that sassy mouth tilted at the corners, and only the dark smudges under her eyes gave away the momentous revelations of the past twelve or so hours.

'Hi,' she said softly.

'How are you?'

The smile wavered a little. 'I'm fine, thanks.'

'Really?'

She nodded. 'Really.'

'Did you sleep?'

She shrugged, her smile slipping a little more. 'Not really.'

'Neither did I.'

Maisie sighed and threaded her hand through the wild ebony strands of her hair, tousled by the early-morning breeze that tugged at them as they walked along the river wall. 'Look, I'm really sorry about Hector—'

'No. No, it wasn't Hector. Not really. He was just the icing on the cake. I was...' What? Fantasising about her? Wishing that he had a right to be involved with her, that they'd made this baby together?

'You were...?' she probed, and he shrugged and laughed a little awkwardly.

'Just a bit restless. It was hot.'

In fact, the sea breeze across the Ness had kept it beautifully cool, but what was a little white lie between friends?

'You should open the windows,' she said guilelessly. 'Then the breeze would cool you.'

'And then I'd hear Hector,' he said. She coloured softly and he almost groaned aloud. Lord, she was gorgeous, and he was going to have to keep a nice, safe, professional distance—starting now.

'Maisie, come and see me tonight, at the surgery. What time do you finish?'

She shrugged. 'I don't know. Why do I need to see you?'

James hesitated a moment. This was difficult.

'There are things we need to consider—things that might threaten your health.'

Her colour disappeared, leaving her pale and visibly shaken. 'I hadn't even thought—you mean HIV?'

'Amongst other things, all of which are far more likely. We should do a urine test to make sure it is just the pressure of your uterus and you don't have an infection, and you need blood tests for all the routine things like haemoglobin, blood sugar and so on, never mind any sexually transmitted infections. You'll need swabs and smears, too, so I'll arrange for a nurse to be there to do those for you.'

She'd stopped walking, but now she started again, just slowly, as if she was in a daze.

'Good grief. I hadn't thought it would be so complicated.'

'And there's also the question of whether you want to keep the baby.'

Again she stopped, but abruptly this time, her eyes widening. 'Keep it? Of course I'm going to keep it!' she said indignantly. 'What kind of a person do you think I am?'

'The sort of person who's been drugged and—well, raped, for want of a better word,' he said gently. 'The other day you were using the word "violated". A lot of people under those circumstances would be desperate to have the baby taken away.'

'No way,' she said firmly, shaking her head to emphasise the point. 'Nobody's taking my baby away from me. And anyway, it's not like I don't have a clue who the father is. I've been thinking—he was a good man, James, highly respected in his field, a brilliant academic, an excellent clinician.'

'Good genetic material,' he said thoughtfully, and wondered why that mattered to her. Almost immediately, he had his answer.

'Exactly. She'll be able to be proud of him, not wonder—'

She broke off, and he pondered her strange choice of words and the use of 'she', not 'it'. It sounded curiously autobiographical.

'And I'm sure it wasn't really like him to do that,' she went on. 'I'm certain that it was just because of the head injury. So it's not as if there's even a reason to consider—'

She broke off, as if she couldn't bring herself to say the word, and he smiled, suddenly realising how glad he was to hear her decision and the conviction behind it.

'Good for you,' he said softly. 'Will your family be able to help you?'

She shook her head, and her eyes clouded over. 'I don't have a family any more. My parents have both died, my mother when I was twelve, my father two years ago. They had cancer.'

'Is that why you thought you had it? Because of family history?' he asked, but she shook her head again.

'Well, possibly, but not because of a genetic link. I'm adopted.'

And her remarks about the baby's father suddenly fell into place.

'So you're all alone.' It wasn't a question, but she lifted her chin as if defending her decision, and determination flashed in her eyes.

'I know it won't be easy,' she said, 'but I'll manage. I'm going to do this, James. I'm going to be a good mother.'

'I'm sure you will,' he said, believing it. This tough, determined young woman had guts to burn, and he felt suddenly irrationally proud of her.

'So—what time tonight?' she asked, as they arrived back at her house and put the dogs in the run.

'Six-thirty? Or whenever. I'll wait for you. Ring the surgery if you're going to be later than that, because I don't want to keep the nurse hanging around.'

She stroked Tango's head absently, reassuring her, and the simple act gave James a warm, fuzzy feeling inside.

Hell. He was getting too involved—and certainly far too involved to continue to act as her doctor. 'Can I talk to Jane Shearer about you?' he asked abruptly, and she looked up, her eyes wide and worried.

'Do you have to?'

He shrugged. 'I just feel— We're neighbours, Maisie. More than that—friends, almost. It's not appropriate.'

'Appropriate? Why on earth not?'

He shifted awkwardly. 'Maisie, you're pregnant. You'll need antenatal care—regular examinations—and I don't think I...'

He saw the moment light dawned, and colour ran hot and swift over her cheeks. She turned away.

'Of course. How silly, I didn't even think about that. Um. Does she need to know everything? It's just...the circumstances are a bit...'

She trailed off, and he concluded, 'Unusual?'

She laughed, a brittle sound, and he realised that for all her courage, she was hanging on by a thread.

'I tell you what. I'll do the first tests, and get a nurse to take any necessary swabs. I'll simply say you're overdue for a smear—that should cover it. And then I'll hand you over to Jane and I'll keep an eye on your notes if you like and discuss anything you're worried about. Will that do?'

She looked up at him, her cheeks a little warm still and her eyes over-bright. 'Thank you,' she said, so quietly that if he hadn't seen her lips move he wouldn't have known she'd spoken.

'My pleasure. Right. If you think the dogs will be OK, I'd better get off to work. What about you? Are you all right to work today? I can give you a sick note if you want.'

She shook her head. 'No. I'm pregnant, not sick. I'll be fine. I'll save my sick leave for when I need it. And anyway, I could do with being busy. Give everything time to settle in my head before I have too much time alone to think about it too much. Thinking won't change it, James, so I'd rather not waste the energy.'

He nodded slowly, then with a reassuring squeeze to her shoulder he turned on his heel and walked swiftly away, before he gave in to the urge to pull her into his arms and kiss her better.

'Kirsten? Are you busy?'

'Maisie? Hi. Are you OK? I tried to ring you last night but you were out.'

'I was with James.'

She almost heard Kirsten's ears prick. 'James? Oh, my God! Mr Body-To-Die-For James next door?'

'Yes. We had supper. Look, can you come round?

I'd come to you but I'm really tired, and I want to talk to you. I've got something important to tell you.'

'I'll be right there.'

There was a click, and the line went dead. Maisie smiled wryly. Kirsten was so predictable. Give her the slightest little hint of mystery and she was in there without hesitation.

It only took her ten minutes to arrive, by which time Maisie had put some popping corn in the microwave and made a jug of coffee. It was decaf, but even full strength wouldn't keep her awake tonight, she was so tired.

The door banged open and shut again, and Kirsten was there, eyes sparkling with curiosity. 'Well?'

'And hello to you, too,' she said with a chuckle. 'Coffee?'

'Mmm. And is that toffee popcorn I can smell? This must be serious.' But the sparkling in her eyes didn't diminish. If anything, it grew brighter, and Maisie suddenly found herself wondering how to say the words.

'It is,' she began, and then Kirsten looked at her— really looked at her for the first time—and the sparkle went.

'Oh, God, Maisie, what is it? What's happened?'

And just like that, the floodgates opened, and she found herself wrapped in Kirsten's slender but comforting embrace.

'Tut-tut, silly girl,' Kirsten said, rocking her, and after the initial flood of tears, Maisie eased out of her arms and reached for a tissue.

No James this time to proffer an immaculately laundered hanky, she thought with a touch of hysteria, and blew her nose vigorously. Kirsten was watching her worriedly, her hand moving up and down Maisie's arm in a comforting gesture.

'Are you OK, Maise?'

'I'm fine. Just—a bit shocked, really. Come on, let's take the coffee and the popcorn and go and sit down.'

Once they were settled on Maisie's old sofa, the popcorn wedged between them and steaming mugs of coffee cradled in their hands, Kirsten fixed her with a searching look.

'OK. Give.'

Maisie shrugged. Where to start?

'Try the beginning,' Kirsten said, reading her mind, and she gave a shaky laugh and tipped her head back against the sofa.

'The beginning. OK. Do you remember, a few months ago, I showed you that thing in the paper about my old college professor?'

'The guy who topped himself in a police cell because he'd been caught drugging some girl?'

'That's the one. We had a laugh about it.'

'Yeah, because you'd been drinking with him a few days before and you said what a lucky escape—'

Kirsten broke off, her eyes widening. 'Oh, God. It happened to you, didn't it? And you've caught something off him—not HIV. Tell me it's not HIV.'

'No. Well, I don't know yet. That's being tested. No, it's worse than that.'

'How can it be worse? Oh, no, you're pregnant!'

Kirsten sat bolt upright, sending coffee and popcorn flying in all directions, and stared at her in horror. 'You are, aren't you? You're pregnant!'

She shrugged. 'So the test said. I went to the doctor, but I was late, and Jane Shearer had gone, but I saw James—'

'James? *Our* James? He's a *doctor*?'

'Yes—not a fat cat from the city at all, so I'm sorry to ruin your illusions,' she said wryly, remembering James's slightly bitter words. 'The antiques are inherited. Anyway, he told me I was pregnant, and I didn't believe him,' she said, leaving out the hideous scene and her temper tantrum. 'So I did a test, to prove him wrong.'

'And it didn't.'

'No, it didn't. That's what I was doing there last night—talking it through, because I just had no idea how it could have happened.'

'You don't remember?'

She shook her head. 'Only drinking with him and feeling sorry for him because his life had gone pear-shaped since the accident.'

Kirsten slumped back against the sofa, crushing popcorn into the upholstery and staring at Maisie, wide-eyed. 'So what are you going to do?'

'What do you mean, what am I going to do? I'm going to have a baby—the first week in November, apparently.'

'Oh, my God. Can I be godmother?'

'Only if you learn to moderate your language,' Maisie teased gently, and Kirsten, the queen of cool, actually blushed.

'God, I'm sorry—there I go again! You'll have to have a swear box.' She fished some of the popcorn out from behind her back and ate it absently. 'So what will you do about work? November—grief, it's already June! That's not so long, really, is it? I'm amazed you don't show.'

'I do.' She stood up, pulled up her top and turned sideways to Kirsten, peering down as she did so and looking in wonder at the gentle swell of her abdomen. Her friend's eyes widened.

'Wow. That wasn't there last week.'

She laughed. 'Oh, yes it was, it was stuck in my pelvis pressing on my bladder and making me pee every five minutes.' Her smile faded. 'It's almost as if, now I know, it's allowed to show—does that sound silly?'

Kirsten shook her head, as much in bewilderment as anything, and stared at Maisie's no-longer-flat tummy as if she couldn't quite take it all in. 'So what have they said at work?'

Maisie pulled a face and plopped back onto the sofa, spilling the rest of the popcorn. 'I haven't told them. What do I say? It was a one-night stand but I don't know who it was? I was drugged? It was an old boyfriend but we aren't seeing each other again? They know I'm not in a relationship.'

'So tell them nothing. Leave them guessing—it's nobody's business but your own.'

'Funny you should say that. It's exactly what James said this evening.'

'So believe us. We can't both be wrong.' She tutted and reached out her hand, rubbing Maisie's arm again in support. 'Are you OK? Really? I mean—that's like rape, isn't it? Don't you need counselling?'

She shook her head. 'No. I'm fine—and, anyway, talking to James is like seeing a counsellor. He's been brilliant but, really, I'm all right. I can't remember it,

I don't know anything about it. It's like it's happened to someone else. At first I felt as if my body had been, I don't know, burgled or something, but now—I know it's silly, but I feel like this is my baby, nobody else's. Just mine.' She gave a little laugh. 'I know it's crazy, but I'm really quite excited, now it's sunk in. Kirsten, I was adopted. I've never had a relative before—not a blood relation. And now I will. It's fantastic.'

Kirsten stared at her in amazement, then a smile broke out on her face.

'You really mean it, don't you? Oh, Maisie, I'm so glad you're OK.'

Kirsten leant over and hugged her, then sat up abruptly and sniffed, blotting her eyes with the backs of her hands and streaking her make-up everywhere. 'Look what you've made me do!' she wailed, laughing, and Maisie smiled and scooped up another handful of popcorn and ate it while Kirsten pulled herself together and scrubbed mascara off her hands.

'So—what now?'

'Now I have to go to antenatal classes and learn how to give birth and how to be a mother, and I have to sort out some kind of maternity leave and part-time stuff for later with my boss, and it's going to be chaos.' Her smile faded. 'I'll need help, Kirsten. I hate asking, but if I need anything...'

'Then ask. Never mind hating it. You just ask. And I don't want to hear that you can cope.'

Maisie laughed, and stood up. 'More coffee?'

Kirsten shook her head. 'No. You need to take your baby to bed. You look bushed.'

'I am bushed. I didn't sleep very well last night.'

That was an understatement. She'd had about an hour of sound sleep before the alarm had rudely woken her at six. After Kirsten had left she put the dogs out, checked that the chickens were all in the run and shut them in. Not that it worked.

She was still one down, a pretty little Light Sussex hen called Helga. She was always going broody, and she suspected that she'd taken herself off somewhere and the fox had got her.

'Poor Helga,' she murmured, and felt the prickle of tears.

For a chicken? Good grief. These hormones were going to be the giddy limit. How was she going to feel when she had to put down someone's beloved dog or horse? It didn't bear thinking about.

Whistling for the dogs, she went back inside, stroked Max, the ginger cat, in passing, and went up to bed, the dogs trailing hopefully behind her.

'Sorry, darlings, not tonight,' she said, and closed the door firmly on their noses. She didn't put the light on, but instead crossed to the window and looked over at James's house. It was ten-thirty, but there was no light on in his bedroom. She could see light spilling out over the lawn at the back of the house, though, and as she stood there, she heard him call Tango.

A minute later the light came on in his room, and he crossed to the window, closed it firmly and shut the curtains. She felt stupidly shut out, and to her disgust her eyes filled with tears.

How ridiculous! She was turning into a watering-can! She got into bed, turned out the light and was asleep in moments.

*   *   *

He had a flea bite.

He couldn't believe it. He'd been scratching his leg in his sleep and, in fact, at one time it had been so bad it had woken him. James glared down at the flayed skin and swore colourfully.

Tango. It had to be—and she'd probably got the fleas from Jodie and Scamp. They'd been shut up together now for two days.

Great. Infested by a vet's dogs! What kind of an advert was that?

Still, he had the morning off today, so he'd take himself off to the vets' and get some spray. But which practice? Maisie had gone off to work ages ago, so he couldn't ask her. That would teach him to have a lie-in!

He looked in the *Yellow Pages*, but it was singularly unhelpful. None of them listed Maisie's name, so he picked one at random and phoned.

'Do you have a Miss McDowell working for you?' he asked, and, of course, he was fielded by a protective receptionist.

'Who's calling?'

'The name's Sutherland. I'm her new neighbour.'

Immediately her tone changed, becoming concerned. 'Is there a problem?'

So she was there. He gave a wry smile. 'No. No problem. I need to see a vet with my dog, so I thought I'd come to her.'

'She's got an appointment free in fifteen minutes. Can you make that?'

'I'll do my best.'

'I'll tell her to expect you, Mr Sutherland.'

The phone went dead before he could ask directions, but he thought he knew where it was. He called Tango, got the car out of the garage and set off, the dog breathing heavily down his neck all the way there. He really, really needed to get a carrying cage or harness, he thought as her tongue swiped wetly across his ear. Or at the least a blanket for the back seat.

'Don't crawl to me, you've got fleas,' he told her sternly, and she grinned at him in the rear-view mirror and looked utterly unrepentant. 'You wait,' he said. 'I'll get Maisie to vaccinate you. That'll teach you.'

He found the practice without difficulty and took his place in the waiting room. A few moments later Maisie came out and crouched down in front of the dog, throwing James a puzzled smile.

'Tango! Hello. What are you doing here?'

'Fleas,' he said expressionlessly, and Maisie looked up again, her eyes brimming with laughter.

'Fleas?'

'So it would seem.'

'Well, we'd better go and have a look.'

She led him through into the consulting room, helped him lift Tango onto the table and got a telling-off from him for picking her up.

'Don't be ridiculous, I have to do my job,' she said dismissively. 'Right, why do you think she's got fleas?'

He hitched up his trouser leg and she winced. 'Ah. Right. OK, I'll check her, but I don't know where she's got them from. Mine haven't got fleas.'

He grunted under his breath, but she must have heard because she shot him a look.

'Mine *haven't* got fleas,' she repeated, and ran her fingers through Tango's coat, brushing it backwards. 'There we are,' she said, and plucked a flea from the dog's back. 'And it's a chicken flea—and before you say it, mine are treated. I wonder where she's got that from?'

'Heaven knows. What's the difference?'

'In the type of flea? Slight but noticeable.'

'Not to my leg,' he grumbled gently, and she laughed and turned to her computer.

'She's not the natural host, so they will migrate onto anything else living to see if it's better. Hence your bites. I'll get you some flea treatment that should sort her out. It'll kill any fleas on her and prevent reinfestation.'

'Not organophosphates?' he asked, checking, and she shook her head.

'No. Not any more.'

'Good.'

She turned back to him, a smile on her face, and was about to speak when the door flew open.

'Maisie, it's David. He's operating, and he says he's feeling really ill. He's dizzy, and he looks awful. Can you come? He wants you to finish up for him, he just can't do it.'

She glanced up at James. 'Would you mind if I abandon you?' she said. 'Kathy will look after you and get you the flea stuff.'

'Of course,' he said, conscious of a ludicrous and quite unwarranted disappointment. 'You go and take over.'

Then he heard a man groan and retch, and his professional instinct kicked in. That wasn't ordinary nausea—not unless the man was a total drama queen.

'Do you want me to take a look at him? He sounds really quite ill.'

Maisie, her face concerned, threw him a grateful look. 'Would you mind?'

He thought of his morning off, already eaten into by the fleas, and the mountain of unpacking and sorting out he'd intended to do, but then the man gasped and groaned again, and he gave a wry smile. 'Of course I don't mind,' he lied, and, Tango in tow, he followed her through the door into the back of the practice.

CHAPTER FIVE

THEY went through a dispensary and what looked like a surgical preparation area into an operating theatre. There, propped up against the operating table, hands braced against the side of it and his eyes firmly shut, stood a man in green scrubs.

His skin matched the colour pretty well, and James didn't like the look of him at all.

'David?' Maisie said, and the man opened his eyes, turned his head a fraction and retched helplessly.

'Lay him down,' James said quickly, and took hold of David's shoulders, easing the man down onto the floor. Someone took Tango away, to his relief, and he knelt down on the floor beside the man and took his wrist.

'Pulse is nice and regular, but a bit fast. David, can you hear me?'

'I can hear you, but I'm not opening my eyes.'

'OK. That's fine. My name's James Sutherland, and I'm a doctor. Can you tell me how you feel?'

'Dreadful. Sick. So, so sick.'

'Is it worse when you move?'

'Yes.'

'Any chest pain?'

'No.'

'Headache?'

'No.'

'And when did it start?'

'This morning—just about an hour ago. It's just got worse and worse.'

'Right. Maisie, can you go out to my car and bring my bag from the boot, please?'

He flung her the keys, and she disappeared through the door and came back again instantly. 'Which car?' she said, and he realised that she'd probably never seen it.

'Dark blue BMW. It's in the far corner of the car park. Just press the remote and you'll see it flash.'

She disappeared again, and he turned his attention back to the vet lying very, very still on the floor.

'David, have you ever had anything like this before, or has anyone in your family suffered from vertigo?'

'No, don't think so.'

'Had a cold recently?'

'No—well, a bit of a sniffle last week. Hell, I feel grim. Is it my heart?'

James squeezed his shoulder reassuringly. 'No, I don't think so. I think you might have either a viral or bacterial infection of the inner ear. It affects the semi-circular canals which control our balance mechanism, hence the dizziness and nausea you're experiencing, and sometimes the cochlea, too, which can affect the hearing in the relevant ear.'

'I had my ears syringed yesterday because I was feeling a bit deaf in one ear,' David said heavily. 'Could that have caused it?'

'Possibly, but it's more likely the deafness was the first sign.'

'You're talking about labyrinthitis, aren't you?' David said, and James heard the dread in his voice.

'Possibly. I have to eliminate any cardiac or cerebral complications just to be certain, but so far that's looking the most likely diagnosis.'

'And it could make me feel this grim?'

'Oh, yes.'

The man swore, softly but succinctly, and James could only agree with him. Labyrinthitis was a horrible condition, the inflammation leading to dizziness and nausea that could last for weeks. Sometimes it could leave the sufferer permanently prone to attacks of dizziness brought on simply by turning the head sharply, but if David wasn't aware of that, there was no way James was going to tell him now. He had enough on his plate.

And grim as it was, it was probably preferable to the other things that could be going on, and which he wanted to rule out as a matter of urgency.

'Can someone call an ambulance, please?' he said, just as Maisie reappeared.

'Ambulance?' Maisie said, her voice full of alarm.

'Just as a precaution,' he said calmly as he opened his bag and took out the portable blood-pressure monitor. 'If it is labyrinthitis, David, you'll need IV anti-emetics for a few days, and that means hospitalisation. Right, I want to check you over now to eliminate any other possibilities. I'll try not to move you too much, but I may have to ask you to do things that unsettle it.'

'Great,' he groaned, and retched again.

Maisie bit her lip, then looked at James. 'Do you need me for anything else?' she asked. 'I really should finish off this dog but I could get Pete to do it.'

James slipped the blood-pressure cuff round David's arm and pressed the start button on the little machine. 'No, you go ahead. I'll shout if I need anything. Oh—have you got ECG facilities?'

'Yes, here,' Kathy said. 'I don't suppose it's the same as yours, but it might work.'

'It should,' David groaned from the floor.

'We'll see.' James was conscious of Maisie moving to the operating table, but he could feel her eyes on him and sensed her concern for her colleague.

'I think I've finished, Maisie. All you need to do is close,' David said, his voice a little slurred.

James didn't like the sound of that. It might have been just plain misery, or it could have been a result of some kind of stroke. Without neurological tests it was impossible to tell, but David's blood pressure was elevated, and that could be significant.

'David, I'd like to test your pupils, but it means opening your eyes.'

'Damn,' he said unhappily, and his lids flickered open, then shut again. 'I can't.'

'Please. I need to do this. I know it's unpleasant.'

His eyes opened again, and he stared fixedly at the ceiling. Quickly, so as to disturb him as little as possible, James flicked the beam of light over his eyes and watched in relief as both pupils contracted equally and rapidly.

Unfortunately, the moving light was all that was needed to trigger another bout of helpless retching.

'Can't you give him an anti-emetic?' Maisie said from her position at the operating table.

'No—not until he's been thoroughly screened for

all other eventualities. Right, I'd like to do that ECG, if possible, please,' he said to Kathy, the vet nurse.

She handed him the leads instantly, and he raised his eyebrows at the little crocodile clips on the end.

'Ouch,' he murmured. 'This might pinch a bit.'

'Just do it,' David said grimly, so James put the leads on his patient's chest.

While he was waiting he found a butterfly and a swab so he could put in an IV line. A few moments later he scanned the ECG readout with relief.

'Well, that looks OK. No indications of any cardiac event or arrhythmia, but I'd need an eight-lead to be sure. David, I'm going to put a butterfly in your hand ready for IV access, OK?'

The man grunted consent, clearly too ill to care any longer what happened to him, and James slipped a band round his arm, flicked up the vein and inserted the needle.

'Anybody would think you'd done that before,' Maisie teased, and he realised she'd finished with the dog and was crouching beside him.

'Just once or twice.' He took advantage of the venous access to do a blood-glucose test, and he'd just ascertained that it was normal when he hear a siren approaching. 'Sounds like your taxi's here, David,' he said calmly, and hoped the journey would be uneventful and smooth. Even getting him into the ambulance was going to be well nigh intolerable, and James didn't envy David one little bit.

Poor bastard, he thought, and was suddenly terribly glad that he'd come in that morning with Tango and had been there when this had happened—not that he'd been able to give him anything to help, for fear of masking another condition, but at least he'd been able to set all their minds at rest about anything more sinister.

Then the paramedics were there, and James was handing over, filling them in and jotting notes hastily as they lifted David onto the trolley, retching violently with every slight movement, and wheeled him out through a side door to the waiting ambulance.

'Do you need to go with him?' Maisie asked, but James shook his head.

'I don't think so. He's in good hands.' He turned to the crew as they closed the doors. 'Thanks, guys,' he said, and then he put his bag into his car and turned back to Maisie, giving her a wry smile. 'I don't suppose you know what happened to my dog?'

Maisie chuckled. 'Yes. She's out the back, being de-flea'd.'

'Ah. Poor Tango.'

'She'll be fine. James, about David—'

'He'll be all right, Maisie. I'm virtually certain it's just labyrinthitis, though heaven knows that's bad enough, but it's better than a stroke or a potentially fatal heart condition. Nevertheless, I'm sorry, Maisie, your colleague's going to be out of action for weeks, if not months.'

'Oh, joy,' she said, rolling her eyes. 'All those extra surgeries and visits. I can hardly wait.'

As if it had suddenly dawned on her that he'd stepped in and taken over on his day off, she tipped her head back and smiled up at him, her eyes appreciative.

'Thank you for looking after him,' she said softly,

and at that moment he would have cheerfully given up the entire weekend just for that one smile.

'Any time. You would have done the same,' he reminded her, but she merely shrugged and gave a little dismissive laugh.

'Right, I do believe I've got a clinic going on,' she said. 'I'd better get back to it before they all give up and go home.'

They headed back inside, and as they walked through the door Kathy looked up from the phone. 'It's Lucy. She's got a horse in a ditch. Can you go over now, please?'

Maisie rolled her eyes. 'Sure, tell her I'll be twenty minutes. Has she called the fire brigade and any other big, strong men she can lay her hands on?'

Kathy relayed the message, laughed and put the phone down. 'She says if she could lay her hands on any big, strong men, she wouldn't be running a livery yard. Oh, and it's not a shire this time.'

Maisie chuckled. 'I'm sure it doesn't matter. Shire horse, Shetland—they're all darned heavy when they're stuck in the mud. Right, ask Pete if he can take the rest of my clients this morning, could you? I'd better get over there.'

She turned to James, cocked her head on one side and studied him with a mischievous little smile. 'How's your pulling power?'

He opened his mouth to make a smart retort, but then she wrapped her surprisingly strong little hand around his upper arm and squeezed, and his words died in his throat.

'Tense,' she ordered, and he obligingly flexed his arm. Her fingers tightened, testing his strength, and macho pride made him tense his biceps even harder to impress her.

'Very impressive,' she said, laughter bubbling in those sparkling caramel eyes. 'Are you busy?'

He looked at her for a second and then gave a rueful little huff of laughter. 'Apparently so. I think I'm pulling a horse out of a ditch.'

'Good man, right answer,' she said, patting him on the arm with a wicked grin and heading for the door. 'Kathy, can you hang onto Tango for us?'

'Sure. She's happy now—she's being cuddled.'

'What a surprise,' James said drily, and followed Maisie out of the door, his arm still tingling from the touch of her hand. He got into the passenger seat of her car, and she cut through the streets to the main road and the A12 intersection at a speed that made his blood pressure shoot up.

'You don't take any prisoners, do you?' he said faintly as she shot through a gap in the traffic and whipped round the roundabout, but she just threw him a grim smile.

'No time to hang about. I have no idea how long it's been there, but time is of the essence. They get exhausted, and if they get trapped around tree roots and sunken debris, they have to be put down on the spot. You can't pull them out. I've heard of horses having their limbs ripped off being towed out of rivers by inexperienced rescuers. I need to be there.'

'I can imagine you do,' James said, his voice full of horror. 'How did it get in the ditch?'

'Don't. They have to drink from it—well, it's a little branch of the Deben, really, not a ditch—but they go in at stupid places. They won't just use the gravel bit with a firm bottom, they get silly. Either the grass is lusher on the bank, or they go the wrong way to drink, but they end up in it sometimes.'

'Isn't that bad management?'

She laughed. 'Probably. It's happens in nature, though, very often, so I try not to judge. Horses can be very stupid.'

They arrived at the livery yard to find it deserted, but it seemed she knew where she'd find everyone. She drove down a track, following the ruts left by something large—a fire engine?

Yes. And it was stuck, right in a gateway. Terrific.

'That's handy,' he said.

'Tell me about it,' Maisie said. 'It means I'll have to run backwards and forwards across the field for everything I need, but hopefully I won't need anything yet. They're over there.'

They scrambled through the fence and ran to see what was going on. They found a knot of people clustered on the river bank, heaving on a rope and issuing instructions and yelling at the horse to encourage it. As they approached the crowd subsided into silence again, and the rope went slack. The horse had moved a fraction, but as soon as the struggling helpers eased off, it slipped back into the sucking maw of the river. Maisie squeezed her way to the front of the group and took in the scene at a glance.

The horse was buried in the mud up to its neck, the only visible part of it the head resting on Lucy's lap, and it was so plastered with mud it was impossible to tell what colour it was. Lucy didn't look much better herself, but she managed a rueful smile of welcome. 'Well, if it ain't the cavalry. Got any ideas?'

'Only the usual. It looks exhausted.'

'He is, poor old boy. Aren't you, Pharaoh?'

The horse was making no effort to free himself, but was simply lying with his head on Lucy's legs and struggling for air, his eyes rolling with fear and a tremor running through him from time to time.

'I brought muscles,' Maisie said, and Lucy ran an appreciative eye over James.

'Good,' she said, and struggled to her feet, holding the horse's head up as she did so. 'Right, let's have another go.'

The helpers took up the strain on the heavy lunge-line knotted through the noseband of the lunging cavesson. It was similar to a head collar, but because it was stronger it was less likely to break under the huge strain. This wasn't the first time they'd all done this, and it wouldn't be the last, Maisie was sure, but at least with experience they'd perfected the art of getting the horses out, and they hadn't lost one yet.

'Right,' Maisie said, grasping the rope, and found her hands being prised off it very firmly, finger by finger.

'I think not.'

'James, don't be silly, I don't have time to muck about.'

He returned her exasperated glare impassively. 'Time is exactly what you have. You're not pulling on this rope—or if you do, I won't, and I'm stronger than you, so which is it to be? You, or me?'

Their eyes locked, and she could see she wasn't going to win this argument before the horse died of hypothermia, and possibly not even then. But only yesterday she'd felt the baby move for the first time,

a real solid kick that couldn't be confused with anything else, and she knew he was right.

She stepped out of the way, and they all took up
the slack again.

'Right, on three. One, two, three!' Lucy said,
scrambling out of the way and adding her weight to
the lunge-line.

'This is hopeless,' a fireman gasped after the third
fruitless attempt. 'We need a vehicle attached to this
line so we don't lose what ground we gain. I don't
suppose we can get one in here, though,' he added,
giving the fire engine a speaking look.

One of the other firemen in his muddy yellow trousers looked acutely embarrassed.

Lucy sighed and rammed her muddy hand through
her once-blonde hair. 'We'll just have to cut down
the fence and drive my pick-up in here,' she said.
'Maisie's right, and the horse is exhausted. He can't
take much more, we have to get him out now.'

'Can't we get a sling under it?' one of the firemen
suggested, but his colleagues soon scoffed him into
silence.

'We've tried before. That horse is enormous.
Getting anything under it is impossible. The bottom
of its ribcage is about three feet down, and I'm not
going in head first!'

'Dig it out?'

'We could have used the winch on the engine, of
course, only someone bogged it down in the gateway!'

More good-natured ribbing, but in the meantime
Maisie was sitting with her legs under the horse's
head, stroking him and checking him over as much

as she could in the limited conditions while someone went to cut down the fence and bring back a vehicle.

'Poor old lad,' she murmured, feeling the base of his ears for cold. They were chilly and clammy, not surprisingly. He must be suffering from hypothermia. As she stroked him and spoke soothingly to him, another shudder ran through him. His heart was pounding, his breathing was laboured and she had a horrible feeling he had taken some water into his lungs.

Not good news. The horse was quite literally at the end of his tether.

'How is he?'

She turned her head at the sound of James's quiet voice in her ear. 'Not good. We have to get him out of here now,' she said firmly, just as Lucy drove up in her pick-up.

'I thought towing them out wasn't an option,' he said, still quietly.

'We aren't going to tow him. We're going to pull him ourselves, but then move the vehicle to take up the slack. It'll be as safe as we can make it.'

She scrambled out from under the horse's head, and Lucy took over the job of supporting it so he didn't drown.

'Right, tie the line onto the towhitch, but I don't want to pull him out with the truck if we can avoid it.'

It was a struggle, but in the end they managed— without Maisie's help, to her total frustration. She had to content herself with holding onto the head collar and encouraging the horse with her voice and her hands.

Slow, steady traction, lots of encouragement and

support for the horse from Maisie and Lucy, and finally his front legs were free and he flailed and struggled his way out onto the bank. They'd pulled him up onto a tarpaulin, and now this was hauled away from the river, horse and all, so that if he staggered when he got up, he didn't fall straight back in.

'Come on, Pharaoh, get up,' Lucy said, tugging on the line, and eventually the poor exhausted horse dragged himself to his feet to a great round of applause and cheering.

He was shivering, a sign Maisie found encouraging. If horses were too cold, they didn't even shiver, and that was much more significant. While Lucy walked him slowly forwards, she watched him for signs of lameness. It was so easy to damage limbs when dragging horses from mud, even if they weren't entangled on anything—in fact, not only limbs, but spine and neck, and Maisie knew that within a couple of days he would be checked over by the equine shiatsu practitioner Lucy used, to sort out any aftereffects of his escapade.

In the meantime she had to get him back up to the yard, hose him off a bit and check him over thoroughly for injuries. 'Can you drive my car back up to the yard, please?' she said to James.

He eyed her levelly. 'Only if you promise not to do anything stupid while my back's turned,' he murmured.

She managed to hold his gaze more or less steadily. 'Stupid? Of course I won't be stupid.'

'That's a matter of opinion,' he muttered, turning away, and she sighed with relief and turned back to the horse.

'Right, let's get Pharaoh back up to the yard,' she said to Lucy.

The woman was studying the horse worriedly. 'You reckon he's OK to walk? I could bring the lorry down. I don't want to cause any further problems, he's a valuable animal.'

No wonder she was looking worried. She'd have to answer to the owner, Maisie thought, who might have plenty to say about her horse being kept in a field with an unfenced river and no other water supply.

'Maybe you need to look at fencing off the muddier stretches of bank,' she said to Lucy as they walked. 'This is the third time—it's beginning to be a habit.'

'Tell me about it,' Lucy muttered. 'The trouble is, the landlord won't pay for the fencing and I can't afford to post and rail it—and, anyway, it's under water for weeks at a time if we get a lot of rain, and it would just wash it out. And I can't afford to waste the grazing, because it's wonderful down here.'

It *was* wonderful—the grass soft and thick and lush, the trees providing shelter from the heat and the flies and the rain, and it was as near as horses could get to being a natural environment.

'Maybe you need an alternative source of water and portable electric fencing,' Maisie suggested.

Lucy snorted. 'Tried that. They knock the water over and then trash the fencing and go in the river anyway.'

'So who do I bill?' Maisie asked, and Lucy sighed.

'Bill me. I'll discuss it with the owner when I talk to her. Just don't find anything awful wrong.'

She chuckled. 'Well, he's looking lucky so far.'

They were walking slowly back up the track, James following at a nice safe distance and watching her, Maisie was sure, like a hawk. No need. Pharaoh was too tired to do more than stumble up the track to the yard, and the most taxing thing Maisie was called upon to do was walk beside him.

In the end, they discovered he'd been lucky. Once he'd been hosed and checked, he had a few minor scrapes but nothing to worry about. The most significant factor was cold, and he was soon rugged up and drying off, with his nose in a bucket of warm mash.

She gave him a shot of an antispasmolytic in case he developed colic, an anti-inflammatory for the inevitable strains and pains and an antibiotic against the possibility of pneumonia, and she left Lucy with a course of antibiotics to inject daily for the next five days.

'I'm bound to be up here in the next few days, so I'll give him a look then unless you're worried. I'm sure you know what to look out for. You might need to hose his legs if they swell or heat, and you could try arnica and witch-hazel gel. In fact, I should put that on his poll where it took the strain of the head collar, and anywhere else that looks as if it's taken a knock.'

'Cheers. Thanks, both of you. I'll see you.'

Lucy went back into the box, her voice soft as she talked to the cold, weary horse, and Maisie and James headed towards her car. She knew Pharaoh would be well looked after now. It was just a shame it had had to happen.

They waved to the firemen, cleaning themselves up

and drinking welcome cups of tea, and climbed wea-
rily into her car.

'Good job you've got seat covers, you're a bit on
the muddy side,' James, frowning at her clothes, and
she remembered she'd been sitting on the river bank.

'Why do you think I have them? Mud's an occu-
pational hazard with large animals. I'll just take them
off and wash them later.' Or not. Probably not. They
seemed to shrug off the dirt pretty well and, despite
not having been allowed to pull the horse, she was
surprisingly weary. The seat covers, she decided,
could wait.

'Thank you for your help,' she said, turning to
James with a smile, and he gave a short, wry laugh.

'My pleasure. I didn't really want to do any unpacking this morning.'

Maisie thought of his house, probably still piled
high with boxes, and felt a twinge of guilt. 'I'll give
you a hand with your unpacking over the weekend,
if you like,' she offered, and he chuckled.

'Feeling guilty, Maisie?' he teased gently, and she
felt herself colour.

'You were a great help,' she told him, which was
entirely the truth, even if it was designed to massage
his ego, and he gave a soft chuckle and settled back
in his seat, folding his arms over his chest and closing
his eyes.

'It'll take more than that.'

'I'll buy you lunch.'

'No time. I've got a clinic at three, and it's already
nearly two. Try again.'

'I'll cook you dinner,' she said without thinking,

and he cracked open one eye and studied her thoughtfully for a second, then closed it again.

'Done,' he said softly. 'Tomorrow night—after
you've helped with the unpacking.'

And Maisie, contemplating the thought of enter-
taining her obviously wealthy neighbour in her own
extremely modest little house, which was in dire need
of her time and a significant cash injection, wondered
why she hadn't just kept her mouth shut...

It was, James realised, the first time he'd been in her
house. He'd brought Tango, on instructions, and the
dogs greeted each other happily and went off, Tango
with her nose to the ground, and left him alone in the
entrance hall with Maisie.

'It's not as grand as yours, I'm afraid,' she was
saying with a crooked little smile, and he had a sudden overwhelming urge to wrap his arms around her
and hug her. Instead, he shoved the chocolates he was
carrying in her direction, and wafted the flowers under
her nose.

Her eyes widened and she sniffed appreciatively.
'Flowers *and* chocolates? You must be feeling guilty
for working me so hard this afternoon,' she teased,
and he chuckled.

'I don't feel in the least bit guilty after dragging
that damned horse out of the river.' He did his own
bit of appreciative sniffing and grinned at her. 'Smells
good. Hope that's for us and not the dogs.'

She laughed. 'My dogs have dry food, but it won't
stop them hanging around hopefully,' she told him.
'It's beef stroganoff—I hope you eat beef?'

'I'll eat anything that smells that good,' he assured

her, following her through into a lovely, light and airy sitting room. It had wonderful views of the river over the low wall that divided it from his garden, and he suddenly understood the reason for the restrictive clause in his contract that prevented him planting anything tall in that position.

'I must take the secateurs to that lot and find the gate,' he said, looking at the ivy that all but swamped it.

'It would be useful with the dogs,' she agreed. 'Here, have a glass of wine.'

'Wine?'

He must have frowned, because she smiled at him knowingly. 'Yes, wine. Don't worry, I'm not drinking and once you've tasted it, no doubt you won't want very much. A grateful client gave it to me.'

He sniffed and sipped cautiously, and then sipped again, savouring the bouquet. Not the best he'd ever had, certainly, but quite passable. 'Thank your client for me,' he told her with a smile. 'Oh, I rang the hospital, by the way. David's improving. They're sure now that it's labyrinthitis.'

'So he'll be off for weeks. Great.'

'Can't you get a locum?'

'Probably. We'll certainly try.'

'Do. You shouldn't be taking on any more than you have to.' Which probably included cooking for him, he thought, his conscience pricking. 'Anything I can do?'

She shook her head. 'No, it's all done. The nice thing about beef strog is it's good and quick. I just put the rice on five minutes ago, so your timing's perfect.'

He tugged his forelock. 'Just obeying orders, ma'am.'

Her smile was disbelieving and very infectious. She went through to the kitchen, and he followed her, noting the tired units, the battered table and chairs and the hole in the vinyl flooring in front of the sink.

'It's my next job,' she told him, as if she'd read his mind. 'I was going to refit the kitchen this summer, but I don't suppose I'll be able to now I'm pregnant.'

'No.' Glancing down as she turned away, he could see that she'd started to show, the smooth round curve of her abdomen outlined by the soft jersey of her T-shirt. Damn. He swallowed the lump that the sight of a pregnant woman so often put in his throat, but it wouldn't go.

Maisie was beautiful. Fit, healthy, her skin glowing with an inner radiance, but he knew that just under the surface lurked a minefield of unresolved questions and health issues.

I feel—is violated too strong a word?

A cocktail of emotions washed over him again—anger, compassion and something he didn't want to look at too closely because, under the circumstances, it was entirely inappropriate.

Damn. James strolled out through the French doors into the garden and dragged in a lungful of the beautiful scented night air.

'What a gorgeous smell.'

'Nicotiana,' she said from behind him, and he turned and found her just there, inches away—close enough to reach out and draw her into his arms and kiss her...

'I'll have to learn something about gardening,' he said lightly, turning away again so he didn't have to look into those warm caramel eyes and be tempted by the soft, full lips below that surprisingly strong and slightly aquiline nose.

'Later. Supper's ready,' she told him, and reluctantly, because sitting over a meal *à deux* with her would inevitably be an exquisite form of torture, he turned and followed her back into the room.

'Thank you for your help today with the unpacking,' he said after they'd taken their places at her simple table and she'd piled his plate with rice and the delicious-smelling beef.

She laughed softly. 'My pleasure. I was dying to get a look at the house anyway,' she confessed, and he shook his head slowly.

'You should have said.'

'When? In between telling you off for leaving Tango alone and discovering I was pregnant?'

He laughed wryly. 'OK, I'll admit it's been a bit of an odd week. So, do you think Miss Keeble would approve?' he asked her, still curious about her benefactor, and Maisie smiled.

'Yes—definitely. Of you, and of the house.'

'And do you?' he asked, and she hesitated.

'Yes,' she said, and it was only later that he realised he hadn't known which of them she'd been talking about—him, or the house.

CHAPTER SIX

'I THINK I've found out where Tango got the chicken
fleas.'

Maisie, in the act of weeding the little bed outside
her sitting-room window, jumped a mile and stood
up, hand on her heart.

'Are you trying to frighten me to death?'

James's crooked grin was appallingly sexy and
made her stupid heart beat even faster. 'Sorry. Want
to come and see?'

She scrambled over the low wall and followed him
round the side of the house to the utility area behind
the coach-house.

And there, tucked down in the woodshed behind a
pile of logs, was Helga, fluffed up and indignant at
their presence, sitting, if Maisie wasn't very much
mistaken, on a clutch of eggs.

'You silly girl,' Maisie chided, and squirmed in
through the narrow gap and grasped the little white
chicken firmly. She was pecked for her pains, of
course, but not hard, and there under the hen were
nine little pale brown eggs, beautifully arranged in a
circle, narrow end in. Maisie put her back on them
and sighed. 'Well, at least she's still alive.'

'She's lucky not to have been eaten by a fox, I
guess,' James suggested, and she nodded.

'She is lucky—but she's been missing about two
to three weeks—which means those eggs are going to

hatch any day now. I'll have to put her in the slammer and chuck the eggs—'

'But they're about to hatch, you said.' He sounded horrified, and she tipped back her head and looked up at him, a slightly hysterical laugh rising in her throat.

'Yes—and absolutely the last thing I need in my little garden is any more chickens, so given a grain of sense I'll put her in solitary confinement on a wire floor and throw away her babies. You, on the other hand,' she added, eyeing his garden meaningfully, 'have room for nine little chicks and their mummy, surely?'

He threw up his hands. 'Oh, no—no, Maisie, not me. I don't do chickens.'

She shrugged and reached for Helga again, ruthlessly calling his bluff. 'OK, I'll just chuck them, then.'

'All right!' His hands were up again, but this time in surrender. 'All right. I'll have the damn chickens. What do I do with them?'

She laughed and straightened up. 'Not a lot. You need a broody run, hay to make a nest, some chick crumbs, some flea treatment which I can give you, plenty of fresh water in a shallow container so they don't drown when they're tiny, and Helga will do the rest.'

He looked utterly bewildered, and Maisie took pity on him. 'I think there might be something round here you can keep them in, unless it's all been cleared out by the builders,' she said.

'No. I had enough on my plate with the house. I thought I'd worry about the garden when I got here, all bar the routine maintenance. I had that done, but nothing else, so whatever was here should be here still. I seem to remember something in the orchard.'

'Right, let's have a look,' she said, and under the apple trees at the far end of the garden she found a little ark almost buried in the long grass. 'Here we go. It's a bit mucky and if you kick it hard enough it'll probably fall to bits, but it'll do for now. It's got a nice little nest area, a wire run safe from the foxes and somewhere under cover for the food and water. Perfect. You just need to scrub it out—'

'Me?'

She turned her hands palms up and smiled at him innocently. 'Of course. They're your chickens now.'

His mouth tightened, and she suppressed a smile and dragged the heavy ark out of the long grass.

At least, she began to, but he prised her fingers off the carrying handle and glared at her.

'I don't think so,' he said firmly, and took hold of it. 'Right, where to?'

Chickens. Chickens, for goodness' sake!

James let his breath out on a sigh and gave the ungrateful Helga a baleful look. If she'd pecked him once, she'd pecked him a dozen times, but now she was de-flea'd and safely installed in her smart new run—because, of course, the other one had indeed fallen to pieces as he'd shifted it and he'd had to go out and buy another one at enormous expense—and the eggs were nestled underneath her on a bed of hay, warmed initially, as instructed by the resident vet and former owner of said chicken, with a hot-water bottle, and he was free to get on with his life.

Huh!

'You'd better be hatching hens, not cockerels,' he

told Helga sternly, 'because otherwise you're going to have to live about four hundred years to pay back the cost of that house.'

She returned his stare coldly, and he shut the end of the run and left her to it.

'All settled?'

He turned and glowered at his neighbour, who was looking fetching in a little pink vest top and shorts. Fetching and pregnant and very, very sexy. All this fecundity, he thought crossly, and rammed a hand through his hair.

'Do you have any idea what henhouses cost?' he said, still reeling from the bill.

She just smiled. 'Look on it as your contribution to animal welfare. Want a cup of tea?'

'I wouldn't mind a cold drink. This weather's getting hotter. I hope you've got sunscreen on those shoulders.' He swung one leg over the wall, then sat there astride it as Maisie went through the newly revealed gate. 'When did that happen?' he asked incredulously.

'Some of us have been busy while you've been messing around with your chickens,' she told him primly, and dragged the gate shut behind her.

'Those hinges need attention,' he informed her, but she just smiled and said, 'Be my guest,' and went on into the house.

'So, how can I tell when the chicks are ready to hatch?' he asked, following her through into the kitchen.

She laughed at him. 'They come out of the shells?' she teased, and he sighed.

'I must be mad.'

This time her smile was kinder. 'No, not mad. You're just a nice man.'

And suddenly it was all worth it.

The heat didn't let up all that week, and they were talking about it going on for the rest of the month. Terrific, James thought. The elderly patients would be struggling to cope, the little ones would be crabby and restless, and the pregnant women would all get high blood pressure.

Which reminded him...

'Jane, can I have a word?'

His colleague sat back at her desk and smiled at him. 'Sure. Come in.'

He shut the door and sat, stretching his legs out and wondering where to start.

'I saw one of your patients last week—Maisie McDowell.'

'Oh, yes, so I gather. She's pregnant.'

He shot her a curious look. 'Word travels fast.'

Jane laughed. 'Not at all. I looked at her notes—I thought I might have to call her in as I'd had to leave promptly, then Patsy told me you'd seen her the night before. She didn't sound very approving.'

James snorted. 'Patsy doesn't approve of anything the patients do. She's too protective of us. Anyway, she's my neighbour—'

'Patsy?'

'No—Maisie. So I don't feel happy to do her antenatal care. Can you do it?'

'Of course. Anything I should know about?'

He thought of Maisie's reluctance to reveal the circumstances of her baby's conception, and shook his head. 'No. She's fit and well—baby's due in November.

I ran a whole batch of bloods and so forth, because she'd been feeling off, but I really think it was just early pregnancy and she didn't recognise it.'

'A surprise, then. Is her partner pleased?'

'I wouldn't know,' he lied. 'She lives alone, as far as I'm aware.' He stood up. 'So, can I leave it up to you?'

'Of course. I'll contact her and invite her to the antenatal clinic. Thanks for looking after her.'

Jane's words gave him an odd tightness in his chest. 'Just doing my job,' he said lightly, and went back to his room. He had an emergency surgery starting in a moment, and calls to make afterwards, and he really didn't need to think about looking after Maisie.

'OK, Mrs Greer, take these three times a day, and remember to finish the course. That really is most important.' He tore the prescription off the printer, signed it and handed it to his patient, then was about to pack up his desk and go on his calls when the phone buzzed and he picked it up. 'Hello?'

'Dr Sutherland, I've got a Mrs Davies in here with her daughter Eleanor. She says she's still got earache and needs to see a doctor. I've told her you've finished, but she really is most insistent.'

He sighed. If only Patsy would stop protecting him.

'That's fine. I'll see her—I always see children, Patsy. Remember that. Can you please send her in?'

He frowned. Elly Davies was ten, and she'd been in earlier in the week with a middle ear infection. It should have been on the mend by now, unless the organism was resistant to the antibiotic he'd prescribed.

She came in with her mother, looking miserable, and he smiled reassuringly at her and indicated the chair. 'Take a seat, Elly. Mrs Davies, why don't you sit here?'

He drew up another chair for the woman, then sat down again and looked at Elly. 'Right, I gather you've still got earache.'

She nodded. 'It's awful. Normally it gets better after a few days, but this time it's still bad.'

'As bad?'

She shrugged. 'Not quite, but it's not better. It's still really sore.'

She sounded a little tearful, but she was obviously being brave and James got out the auriscope and checked her ear as gently as he could.

'Your eardrum's still very inflamed,' he said. 'Have you had a temperature?'

'Yes—it was thirty-eight last night,' Mrs Davies said.

He took it in the other ear—a simple and quick procedure these days, taking only seconds—and found it was still elevated.

'OK, Elly, I think I might have to change your antibiotics. I haven't got your notes in here—can you remember what it was?'

'Pen-something,' Elly said, and her mother produced the bottle.

'Here. I brought it with me.'

James took the bottle and glanced at it, then looked again. The label printed in the surgery dispensary said penicillin 250 mg in 5 ml, but the manufacturer's label on the bottle said 125 mg in 5 ml. Half the strength.

'Elly, I'm sorry, there seems to have been a dispensing error,' he said, frowning at the bottle. 'I wrote you up for the full strength, and you've been given the strength that would be appropriate for a much younger child.'

'Is that why it hasn't worked?' Elly asked, and he nodded.

'I think so. I'm really sorry. I'm almost certain that's what's happened, and I'm also pretty sure this is the right antibiotic for the job. Is it feeling *any* better?'

'A bit—just not as much better as it usually is by now.'

'Is that just carelessness?' Mrs Davies asked, an edge to her voice, and James shrugged slightly.

'I don't know, Mrs Davies, but rest assured I shall find out. It won't have done her any harm, though, thankfully, apart from the delay in her recovery which I'm really very sorry about. But it's an easy mistake to make.'

'There shouldn't be mistakes,' the woman said emphatically, a fact James heartily agreed with.

'Don't worry. It will be looked into. In the meantime, I'll take this, if I may, and get you a course of the right strength from the dispensary myself. You should notice a definite improvement in twenty-four hours, Elly. If you don't, I'd like to know.'

Mrs Davies stood up. 'Don't worry, Dr Sutherland, you will.'

He didn't doubt it for a minute.

James studied the rota, and found that Patsy had been on that night.

She worked not only as receptionist but also part-time as a relief dispenser, and he knew he'd have to talk to her, but it was one confrontation he wasn't looking forward to. The woman was difficult at the best of times.

He spoke to Jane, and they decided to talk to her together, since Jane knew her better.

Patsy, however, was anything but difficult. She was flustered, panicky and very upset, and they ended up comforting her.

'I can't believe I made such a stupid mix-up,' she said, wringing her hands. 'I mean, it could have been really important.'

'It *was* really important,' James pointed out. 'That child has been suffering unnecessarily for another three days because she had the wrong strength medication.'

'But at least nobody died,' Patsy said, the hand-wringing getting worse, and Jane intervened.

'No. Nobody died, but I wouldn't want you to underestimate this, Patsy. It could quite easily have been a fatal error had the drugs been different. You really must take more care.'

'I'm sorry,' she said, her eyes welling up again. 'I'll be very, very careful in future—if I have a future?'

Jane sighed quietly. 'Of course you have a future, Patsy. Everybody makes mistakes—but since you mention it, I've also been concerned about you vetting our patients at Reception and deciding for yourself whether or not they need to see us. Several people have mentioned it to me, and I think James has found the same thing.'

He nodded. 'This morning, for instance. If Mrs Davies hadn't been so insistent, I might not have seen Elly until tomorrow, and her ear by then might have been much worse,' he said, a little pointedly, and Patsy looked even more uncomfortable.

'But you're all so busy.'

'Patsy, that's what we're here for. We need to know if someone asks for us,' Jane said gently. 'You shouldn't be making clinical decisions. If there's a doctor in the building and someone says their visit is urgent, you need to take details and ask us when we want to see them. You aren't here to protect us from our patients.'

The woman nodded, still upset, and went back to her position at the desk, leaving Jane and James sitting in the office exchanging speaking glances. 'You know what'll happen now?' Jane said softly.

'Absolutely. We'll be consulted about every broken nail—but at least something important won't get missed, and with any luck she'll be a bit more careful in the dispensary. I wonder how many other mistakes there are out there going undetected?'

'Don't.' Jane shuddered and stood up. 'Oh, by the way, your Maisie's results are back. Everything's normal, you'll be glad to know.'

He was. He hadn't realised he was so wound up about it, but he felt the tension go out of him like air out of a balloon, and smiled at Jane. 'Thanks. I'll tell her.'

'Good. Right, I have to go. My husband's got clients coming for dinner, and I have to be there and look charming.'

'And cook?' James asked, worried about the lines of strain around her eyes, but she just laughed humourlessly.

'Hardly. I put my foot down about that and we get it catered. All I have to do is be there, but it's pretty frequent and frankly sometimes I could do without it. That's why I had to go when Maisie McDowell was late—we had a private view to attend. The wife of a client. Politics. I hate it.'

James laughed. 'You and me both. If I'm told something's politically correct, I'm almost tempted to do the other thing just for the hell of it.'

'If it was for me, I would,' Jane said, 'but it's for Michael, and I love him. So I do it—but sometimes it's really hard, juggling work and home commitments.'

James sat back, studying her openly. 'Have you had a well-woman check recently?' he asked.

'Worried about my blood pressure?' she said wryly. 'Don't worry, James, it's fine. I just feel a bit stretched two ways and thin in the middle, if you know what I mean. Anyway, must fly. See you tomorrow.'

'OK, but, Jane? Any time I can help by taking something over for you, let me know.'

She frowned. 'That isn't fair, James. I couldn't do that.'

'Yes, you could. I'd rather cover the odd surgery or clinic for you than have you burning out and deserting me altogether because you're trying to do too much. And anyway,' he added with a grin, 'I'm sure I'll get my own back at some time. I'll give you one of my heartsink patients. That should make you feel better about it.'

Her eyes softened, and she smiled back. 'Thank you,' she said quietly. 'I'll bear it in mind, just in case. Now I really must go.'

He glanced at his watch, surprised to see that it was nearly seven. Amazingly he had no calls to make as duty doctor, and any that came in after seven would be referred directly to the on-call co-operative that all the local practices were a part of.

Which meant he was off the hook.

He grabbed his bag and headed for the door. He had to see Maisie, to tell her about her results. If he hurried, he'd be in time to walk the dogs with her along the river. There'd be a nice cooling breeze at this time of the evening, and they could stroll along to the quay and maybe have a drink at the pub on the way back. It would be lovely there by the water.

His step lighter, he locked up the surgery, hurried towards his car and drove home, but to his surprise Maisie and the dogs were in his garden.

'Your chicks are hatching,' she told him with a smile. 'You've got three so far.'

The walk forgotten, he went with Maisie round to the little henhouse and peeped in through the end door. He could hear the high-pitched cheeping of the chicks, extraordinarily loud for such tiny things, and poking out from under one wing he saw a tiny yellow head, the little beady eyes watching him.

Absurdly, he realised he was excited.

They're just chickens, he told himself in disgust, but Maisie's eyes were bright and he gave up and let himself go with the flow.

'Aren't they cute?' She straightened up. 'Come on, we need to leave her in peace. We'll go for a walk and check her when we come back. It might take until tomorrow for them all to hatch, and then in the late morning she might bring them out into the run.'

As they walked along the river wall, the cooling breeze tugging at their clothes, James wondered at the easy way she'd included him in the walk, just assuming he'd be coming. As, of course, he would. They'd fallen into a routine with astonishing ease, and the dogs seemed perfectly content with the arrangement.

And not only the dogs, he thought, strolling contentedly beside Maisie as she talked about a cat she'd operated on earlier that day to remove a tumour.

'It was horribly complicated, and under any other circumstances I would have given up, but this little cat's been such a fighter, and her owner's all alone and would be devastated if she died now, after all that's gone before. So I went in and did what I could, and to my relief I managed to get it all without killing the cat or destroying any vital nerves. Amazing.'

She was. He smiled at her, a stupid lump in his throat, and for two pins he would have scooped her up in his arms and kissed her, but he couldn't.

Not now. Not yet. She was still so vulnerable. And he hadn't told her about her blood tests, he realised.

'Your results came back today,' he said without preamble, and she stopped dead and looked up at him, her eyes suddenly fearful.

'And?'

'And everything's fine. You're OK, Maisie. You're in the clear.'

Her shoulders dropped, and without warning she burst into tears and he found her in his arms.

'Shh,' he murmured, rubbing her back soothingly and rocking her gently against his chest. Lord, she was tiny, and he could feel the small, firm swell of her abdomen against his body. And then, without warning, he felt the baby kick, and the lump in his throat grew to the size of a grapefruit and threatened to choke him.

He abandoned his plans for walking to the quay,

and instead eased her out of his arms, slung one arm around her shoulders and turned her towards home.

'Come on,' he said gently. 'We'll go home and cook something nice to celebrate.'

He was only being kind, Maisie told herself. It didn't mean anything. He was just being James.

He plonked her down on the sofa in his kitchen, and while he cooked supper she sat there with Tango's head on her lap and Jodie and Scamp curled up on the other sofa as if they owned it, and they drank her health in freshly squeezed orange juice, and then toasted Helga and the chicks. And then after supper, because it was still light, they took another peek at Helga and Maisie pulled out four more shells from under her.

'That's seven,' she said, and James chewed his lip thoughtfully and asked if she could tell the sex.

She laughed and shook her head. 'No—not easily. It's incredibly difficult.'

'So how do commercial producers supply day-old chicks for the egg industry?' he asked.

'Sex-linking,' she said promptly. 'Certain hybrid crosses have different-coloured hens and cockerels, so it's virtually impossible to get it wrong. Otherwise you have to wait until you can see the difference. And they tend to get the egg colour from the father, so your hens should lay the most wonderful dark chocolate brown eggs.'

'Like the ones you've been giving me?'

She smiled. 'Exactly.'

He cocked his head on one side and studied her thoughtfully. 'Are you by any chance a chicken fancier?' he said, with only a trace of humour in his voice, and she laughed and stood up.

'No. I am not. I am, however, a vet, and I'm called upon to know such trivia.'

'Right.'

'Besides which,' she continued with a grin, 'the chickens are quite funny and they have very definite characters.'

'Mmm,' he said, sounding unconvinced.

'Why did you want to know about the sex of the chicks?' she asked, wondering if, when push came to shove, he'd be able to wring the necks of the boys.

'I was thinking of selling the eggs to cover the cost of the chicken house,' he told her, and she felt a bubble of laughter rising out of control in her chest.

'Not a chance,' she told him frankly. 'You'll barely break even with the food, and anyway they'll need a bigger house once they've grown up. You've got eight chickens now, James—and by tomorrow you might have ten.'

'Good grief,' he said, as if it was only just dawning on him what he'd taken on.

'Look on the bright side,' she said cheerfully. 'The other two might not hatch.'

But they did. Or sort of. The eighth struggled out of the shell in the morning, moments after Helga had left the nest, and James squatted down at the end of the house and studied the tiny wet chick cheeping furiously. Helga was ignoring it, so he helped it out into the run and it went to her and snuggled under her wing, and he smiled and looked forlornly at the last egg.

And it was cracking! There was a hole in it, but

without Helga to keep it warm he knew it would die. It was still alive, cheeping and struggling, and of course Maisie was nowhere to be found. 'Let me give you a hand,' he said, and chipped away a little of the shell, but to his horror the membrane inside the shell started to bleed, and he realised that chicks must have a mechanism to cut off the blood supply to the membrane, a bit like mammals cut off the blood to the umbilical cord once they take their first breath.

And the little chick hadn't cut off that blood supply, and now, because of his interference, it might die.

'I'm sorry, little chick,' he said softly, disgusted at himself for being so sentimental. He wasn't even a vegetarian! But the little chick was lying there in his hand, half in and half out of the shell, still cheeping. With a heavy heart, but realising that it was the chick's only chance, James freed it from the remains of the broken shell.

The membrane bled a little more, and the chick was freezing in his hand, but still quite definitely alive. He was standing staring at it and wondering what the hell to do now when Maisie appeared.

'What's up?'

'The last chick,' he said, and told her what he'd done.

She tsked at him and looked at it. 'Poor little mite. You need to warm it up or it'll die. It'll probably die anyway, but you've got more than enough.'

'Hey! This is my chick, I can't let it die,' he said, fiercely protective, and caught the laughing glint in her eye.

'So stick it in your boxers to warm it.'

'It'll fall out of the leg,' he said, not fancying the

thought of the chick in his underwear, but she still had that twinkle in her eye.

'Not if you're wearing the jersey ones,' she said.

He tipped his head on one side. 'Have you been spying on my washing line?' he said accusingly, and she chuckled.

'Hardly spying. It's outside my bedroom window. I can't miss it.' Maisie reached out her hands. 'Here, give it to me, I'll stick it in my bra.'

'What?' Damn, his voice sounded strangled to his ears, but he handed her the chick and watched in fascination and envy as she took the little chick and nestled it inside her vest top.

'Oh, it's cute! Look,' she said, leaning forwards, but all he could see were the smooth, pale globes of her breasts criss-crossed with faint blue veins, and he discovered he didn't give a damn about the chick. He just wanted to bury his face in there between her breasts, exactly where the chick was, and kiss her smooth, pale skin until she cried out.

'Don't suffocate it,' he advised, turning away before she could see his reaction.

'As if,' she snorted, and followed him back to the house. 'If you make a little bed from a box filled with shredded tissues, you could put it in the airing cupboard. Of course, if the Aga was going you could put it on that.'

'If the Aga was going we'd all be dead of heatstroke,' he said drily. 'Here's a box. Make what you like, I'm making tea. Want one?'

It lived. After all the angst and trauma, he tucked it into the little nest box under Helga before he went to bed, and in the morning he discovered it was alive and well, if a little shaky on its pins.

And so he had ten chickens, and he found he was curiously happy. Tango thought they were fascinating, and so did he, and they crouched there for ages watching the tiny little things scratching at their mother's side, and he thought about the tiny bleeding chick in Maisie's bra and wanted to kiss her for saving its life.

Well, he wanted to kiss her for all sorts of reasons, and very few of them were to do with the chick, but she needed a friend more than she needed him coming on to her like a sex-crazed adolescent, he told himself, and so dusting off his knees he found Tango's lead, put her in the car, drove to Rendlesham Forest and took her for a long walk in the woods.

There were two advantages to that. One, it was cooler.

And, two, he wouldn't run into Maisie.

He couldn't get back quick enough.

CHAPTER SEVEN

IT WAS a time for growing, Maisie decided.

The crops were growing in the fields, James's chicks were growing—even, amazingly, the one she'd helped him warm up after Helga had abandoned it—and perhaps most amazing of all, her baby was growing. She was now twenty-one weeks pregnant, and there was no way she could hide it any more.

On the last Friday in June, just under a month since she'd found out she was pregnant and three weeks since his dramatic collapse, she went to visit David. She hadn't seen him except for a brief visit more than a fortnight earlier while he'd still been in hospital and not really paying much attention, and when he saw her, his eyes widened.

'My God. It's true, then.'

She gave him a wry smile. 'Yes, it's true. I was going to tell you, but you conked out on me, and I thought you might have had rather more important things to think about for the last few weeks than a junior colleague.'

He started to shake his head, but thought better of it. 'Nonsense,' he said instead. 'Nothing comes before the health and welfare of my team.'

She laughed. 'You're a sweet liar. How are you?'

His own laugh was hollow. 'Oh, better than I was. Please thank your friend. He was very kind.' David looked pointedly at her bump. 'Is he...um...?'

He trailed off, obviously at a loss for words, and Maisie helped him out. 'Anything to do with this? No. He's my neighbour, and a friend. That's all.'

'Pity. Nice guy.'

'Yes, he is,' Maisie agreed, but she didn't want to think about it too much, because it was pointless.

James seemed to be avoiding her.

Ever since the chicks had hatched, he'd been a little more distant. Busy, slightly remote—nothing specific, really, but she just had that feeling. And yet she found things had been done as if by magic, little things that helped her.

Things like mucking out her chickens, and clearing out the dogs' run, and oiling the hinges on the gate, and sweeping up the petals from her drive when the wind had torn them off one of the rose bushes one blustery day.

James walked the dogs every other day at lunch-time, and took them out in the morning, and in return she walked them in the evening if she was home before him.

Gone, though, were the lovely, companionable walks they'd shared in the first week or so, and she realised she missed them. Ridiculously.

'Like that, is it?' David said softly, and she came back down to earth with a start.

'I'm sorry?'

'You and the good doctor—James, wasn't it?'

'James Sutherland—and, no, it's not like that. It's not like anything.'

'If you say so,' he murmured, and closed his eyes. 'I wish everything would stop sliding off the horizon.'

'Are you still giddy?'

He laughed. 'Just a bit. I can't walk on my own, I can't stand—I can't even go to the loo without help. That really is the pits.' He opened his eyes again and looked at her, and she could see the frustration and worry in his eyes. 'It's going to be weeks, Maisie. Are you coping all right without me?'

'Mmm. It's great, actually. We get to the chocolate biscuits before they're all finished, and there isn't anyone standing over us telling us he wouldn't have done it like that.'

'I don't!'

'Not often,' she relented, smiling. 'But you do eat all the chocolate biscuits.'

'Pete said you've got a locum starting on Monday.'

'We have. She's just qualified, and she wants to work for two months to earn some money before she goes travelling—she didn't have a gap year and she's going to have one now. That could fit in really well.'

'Pete seemed to think she was rather nice.'

Maisie blinked and stared at him. 'Really? That sort of nice?'

'Indeed.'

She laughed out loud. 'I thought he was immune.'

'So did he. Watch this space.'

'Absolutely,' she said. 'Of course, she might not be interested in him. It happens.'

Had there been something give-away in her voice? Maybe, or maybe David was just good at reading between the lines. Whatever, he reached out his hand and wrapped his fingers around hers in an uncharacteristically personal gesture, squeezing them briefly before releasing her. 'Don't despair of James,' he said gruffly. 'If the man isn't a complete fool, he'll realise what a treasure you are, Maisie.'

'David, I told you—'

'I know what you told me. And everything may be sliding off the edge of the world, but I can still see what's at the end of my nose.'

She sighed. 'David, he's not interested. Please, just leave it.'

She remembered the grapes she'd brought him, and produced them with a flourish to distract him. 'Here— they're washed, so you can eat them now.'

'Or you can.'

She grinned. 'We'll share. Is there a bowl any-where?'

'Try the kitchen, and if you can't find anything, ask Ann. She's pottering in the garden with the rab-bits. In fact, call her in and we'll have tea.'

'I can't stop that long,' Maisie said regretfully. 'I've got consults starting again at three, and we're up to our eyes. I thought I'd just come and tell you not to bother to hurry back.'

He snorted. 'Like I can.'

She hugged him because, all things considered, he was a wonderful boss and she was very fond of him, and he patted her back a little awkwardly.

'You take care of yourself and that baby, you hear?' he said a little fiercely. 'I don't want you doing anything dangerous. Anything too heavy or unpre-dictable—any large-animal stuff—get Pete to do it.'

'Pete hates the large-animal stuff, and he's terrified of horses,' Maisie reminded him. 'You'll just have to get better soon, and until then, if I feel it's too much for me, I'll send the locum.'

He laughed. 'Sounds like a good idea.'

She plucked a grape from the bunch and popped it in her mouth. 'Right, I'm off. You take care of yourself, and do what Ann tells you. It'll be good training. You might come back civilised.'

'Not a chance!'

They both turned to look at Ann in the doorway, and although she was laughing, Maisie could see the lines of strain around her face.

'Ann! Hello—how lovely to see you.'

'Hello, yourself. Got time for tea?'

She shook her head. 'No, but I'll come another time. We haven't had a chat for ages. How are all the rescued rabbits?'

'Multiplying. It's that time of year, isn't it? People go on holiday and they can't find anyone to look after them, and they know I won't turn them away. Come on, I'll walk you to your car.'

Maisie waggled her fingers at David and followed Ann out to the car, sensing that she wanted to talk.

'So, how is he, really?'

'Awful. So, so dizzy. They're sure it was definitely labyrinthitis, but until they'd run all the checks and done an MRI scan there was still an element of doubt, and I know he can be opinionated and difficult, but when I thought I might lose him...'

Her eyes filled, and she sniffed and gave a ragged laugh. 'It's strange how you realise you love them when you'd almost forgotten that you ever did. And then, just to punish me for loving him, he turns into the world's worst patient and I could kill him anyway!'

Maisie laughed and hugged her. 'Poor you. Is anybody giving you a break?'

'Oh, yes, my sister and his sister are being very kind, but I still feel guilty. Don't worry about me, I want to talk about you. What's this all about, Maisie?' she asked, looking pointedly at her growing bump. 'You are a dark horse. I didn't know there was anyone on the scene.'

Maisie lowered her eyes and shrugged. She hated lying to her friends and colleagues, but she just couldn't face telling them the whole truth.

'Just someone I used to know,' she compromised. 'It was a one-off.'

'And is there any possibility...?'

This one she could at least answer honestly. 'No. There's no possibility of us getting together. I'm having this baby on my own, and I'm really excited and happy about it, so don't feel sorry for me. It's the best thing to happen to me for a long, long time. Maybe ever.'

'Then I'm really glad for you, and if there's anything I can do, let me know.'

She grinned. 'There is. You can get your husband well and send him back to us, but only when he's really better. The last thing we need is him overdoing it too soon. Anyway, we've got a locum starting on Monday, someone Pete's found.'

'Yes, I've heard all about her. She's going to stay in the flat over the practice. If I can get away I'll give it a thorough clean before the weekend. Don't want to put her off before she even starts!'

As Maisie drove off, she watched Ann in the rear-view mirror. Ann lifted her hand to wave, then turned away, her shoulders drooping. Poor woman. Still, hopefully it wouldn't be too much longer before David was back on his feet and she got her life back. There were countless people in that situation all the time. How did they cope? Badly, she suspected, and wondered how she'd manage if she had a disabled child.

'You'll do your best, and love it anyway,' she told herself fiercely, and went back to the surgery, took her clinic and drove home, to find a note on her door from James.

'Got the dogs. Bit worried about Tango. Can you come round? J.'

She had been looking forward to crawling into a nice cold glass of something refreshing and lying on the sofa watching television for a few minutes while something instant was nuking in the microwave, but for James to mention his concern on the note sounded serious.

The tabbies were rubbing round her legs and clamouring for supper, so she let them in, threw some dry food into their dishes and went round to see James.

Through the beautifully painted and smooth-swinging gate. Amazing. He'd been busy again, she realised, looking at the paint on her fingers, and she glanced at the chicks on the way past and did a mild double-take. They were getting their feathers, and at almost two weeks old were at least three times the size they'd been.

'Helga, you're such a clever girl,' she said, and went to knock on the door just as it swung inwards to reveal James, a worried smile on his face.

'Hi. Thanks for coming round. I hope you didn't mind me asking you. I don't like to take advantage, but—'

'Any time. It's fine. What's wrong with her?' she asked, patting her own dogs absently and looking at Tango for any sign of a problem.

There was nothing immediately obvious. Tango was wagging her tail and greeting her as lovingly as usual, but there was perhaps a slight lack of her usual exuberance. Maisie crouched down and fondled her gently. 'What's up, Tango?' she murmured, checking her eyes for brightness.

The left one was a little weepy, but that wasn't what had worried James.

'She can't seem to eat anything hard,' he said. 'I gave her a biscuit and she cried out when she bit it, and dropped it and ran away.'

'Really? Tango, come here, let me look at your mouth,' she said, and tried to prise open the dog's jaws, but as soon as they were open about an inch, she yelped and ran away.

Maisie sat back on her heels and stared at the dog in consternation. 'I wonder what's wrong. Has she been chewing sticks?'

'She's always chewing sticks,' James said. 'I never throw them for her, but I think my sister did. Why? Do you think she might have hurt her mouth on one?'

'Possibly,' she said slowly. 'I don't know. It might be just a little sore, or she could have strained the jaw joint or pulled a muscle playing with the others, or there could be a bit of stick jammed across the roof of her mouth. There are all sorts of possibilities, but until I can get her mouth open I can't begin to tell.'

'She just won't open it,' he said. 'I've tried, and I got the same reaction you did, only I don't think I got as far as you.'

'Let me try again. Can you hold her? I need to make sure there isn't a stick wedged up there.'

He knelt down, restrained the trembling dog between his knees and held her still while Maisie talked gently to her and coaxed her to open her mouth. She only opened it a fraction of an inch, but it was enough to see that there was no stick jammed across her palate. She didn't push it any further, though, but released her and went back to the academic exercise of eliminating possibilities.

'Is she eating and drinking?'

'Soft food—I gave her some rice and chicken, and she managed that, and she's drinking all right.'

'And she's not drooling.' Maisie sat back and sighed. 'Oh, Tango, my love, what's wrong with you, babes?' she murmured, and the dog wagged her tail and nuzzled Maisie trustingly.

'So what now?'

'Now we watch her,' Maisie said. 'You might find by the morning she's fine.'

'I hope so. I've got a surgery at eight-thirty.'

'So have I. I could take her with me if you like.'

'Let's see,' he said, and then tipped his head on one side and smiled ruefully. 'I bet you haven't eaten.'

'How did you guess?'

He laughed and got to his feet, then held out his hand to pull her up. She had no choice but to put her hand in his, and the warmth and strength of his touch just served to underline how much she'd missed spending time with him in the last week or two.

Had he changed his mind? Realised what a treasure she was, in David's words?

Apparently not. As soon as she was on her feet, he released her and turned away, washing his hands before opening the fridge and rummaging through the contents as if his life depended on it.

'Bacon and eggs?' he suggested. 'I seem to have eggs coming out of my ears.'

She chuckled, putting away her disappointment and taking the moment at face value. 'Funny, that,' she said, drying her hands. 'Your fridge must look like mine. And, yes, bacon and eggs would be lovely. Thank you.'

'Here, put your feet up and drink this,' he said, handing her a glass beaded with condensation.

'Oh, that looks good.'

'Spring water with cranberry and orange juice.'

He was trimming the bacon with surgical precision, and she went and sat down so she didn't have to watch those long, strong fingers working. He had beautiful hands—powerful and yet capable of great tenderness. She'd seen him cradling the tiny chick, holding it safe. Was that how he'd hold her? How would those hands feel on her body?

Gentle. Gentle and persuasive, she thought, and closed her eyes, stifling the moan of need that rose in her throat. If only he was interested in her as anything other than a friend, but if he was, he would have made it clear by now.

No, there was nothing between them, as she'd told David, and that reminded her.

'I've got a message for you from my boss,' she said, deliberately keeping her voice light. 'He asked me to thank you.'

'Oh. My pleasure. How is he?'

'Grim. Still dizzy, can't walk unaided, driving his poor wife mad. I can't imagine he's an easy man to look after. He's fit and healthy and used to doing things his own way. He wouldn't take inactivity lying down, so to speak,' she said, and James chuckled.

'I can understand that. I'd go demented having to rely on someone else for everything.'

'I was wondering how I'd cope with a disabled child,' Maisie said suddenly, and he stopped in the act of lowering the bacon into the pan and looked at her keenly.

'Are you concerned that it might be?'

She shrugged. 'Not really. I haven't thought about it much, but it occurred to me after I saw how David's wife was struggling, and that's just short term. I'm certainly not dwelling on it, and if it happens, it happens. I'll deal with it then.'

'Would it make a difference if you knew? There's a new diagnostic test that assesses your risk factor for Down's and compares it to the norm for your age. Would you like to have the test? It's non-invasive and not conclusive, like amniocentesis, but there isn't any risk to the baby from it.'

She shook her head. 'Seems pointless, and anyway I'm young and fit. If it happens, it happens. One bridge at a time.'

He nodded. 'I agree. How many rashers?'

* * *

Tango was worse in the morning. Her eye had streamed all down her cheek, and when James looked down on the top of her head, her eyeball had been pushed forwards by almost a centimetre.

He took her straight round to Maisie, and she looked down at the dog and tutted softly.

'Poor baby. James, I think I need to take her in with me. I don't like the look of that eye at all, and I have to warn you, she might lose it. Whatever's going on needs urgent investigation.'

He nodded, the thought of Tango losing one of those beautiful brown eyes gutting him. 'Sure. Do whatever you need to do. Don't worry about the cost.'

'I'm glad you said that. If she needs to go to Newmarket for specialist surgery, it will run away with the money. I'll get an X-ray of the area and we'll see what we're dealing with, and then I'll go from there. Shall I ring you?'

'Can I come and observe?' he asked, suddenly very worried for Tango and realising that, his sister's dog or not, he'd become ridiculously attached to her. And anyway, he wanted to know what was going on as much as Maisie did.

'Of course, but I thought you had a surgery.'

'I do,' he said, wishing he could cancel it. 'I should be finished by eleven, though. What time will you look at her?'

'Probably around then. We've got a clinic all morning, and then we'll have a few emergencies to deal with. James, you can trust me,' she said, and he wondered if she felt that he didn't.

'I know that,' he said, hoping she believed him, and so he said it again for emphasis. 'I know I can trust you, but I'd still like to see what you find. It might make it easier to explain to my sister.'

Maisie nodded, then took Tango's lead. 'I'll take her now. Has she had anything to eat or drink?'

He shook his head. 'No. I took away the water last night, because I had a feeling this might happen. Is there anything I can do for you now before I go?'

'Walk the dogs and feed my chickens?' she said with a smile, and he felt his heart lurch.

Lord, she had a beautiful smile. If only...

'Fine. You go. I'll see you as soon as I can get away. Start without me if you have to.'

'OK.'

He watched them go, then quickly grabbed her dogs and went for a run along the river wall, then fed the chickens and arrived at the surgery with only two minutes to spare.

'Dr Sutherland, thank goodness you're here,' Patsy said. 'There's a man to see you. He's most insistent, and he wasn't very polite.' She lowered her voice. 'I think he might be an addict. He's in the waiting room—the one with the tattoos on his face. I've taken the liberty of putting him first on your list, because he's a little bit on the high side, if you get my drift.'

He did, the moment he entered the waiting room. The smell hit him like a brick wall, and he took the man through to the surgery, opened the window and sat him down.

Or tried to. He was twitchy, though, and produced a dog-eared prescription and a medical card so scruffy and defaced it was hard to read. 'I've got a letter from my last doctor,' he said, and pulled an envelope in only slightly better condition from his pocket and handed it to James.

Needless to say it had been opened, but he pulled the letter out and unfolded it, scanning it quickly. It stated that the man was an addict, that he was on methadone 30 ml daily, that he needed to be given it daily and supervised while he drank it.

It was from a GP in Essex who James had never heard of, so he buzzed through to Patsy and asked her to phone the surgery. Moments later he was put in touch with the GP who'd been dealing with the addict in the past.

'Oh, you've got Lenny. He's a bit wild. Watch him. He's not very trustworthy, and he'll take it all at once if you give him more than one day at a time. The only exception is the weekend, and he's normally screaming for it on Monday because he has both days in one hit and then gets desperate, according to the pharmacy who've been dispensing his methadone. Where will he get his supplies?'

'Here,' James said. 'It's a dispensing practice.'

'Then watch him, and make sure it's thoroughly secured. Good luck. I'm only too happy to get rid of him. Oh, and get him to sign a contract.'

'Right.'

James cradled the phone and looked at Lenny thoughtfully.

'So. You're Leonard Price, is that right?'

'Don't call me that. I hate it. Lenny,' he said, rubbing his hands up and down his arms. 'So, can I have some stuff?'

'I'll make sure you have enough for today and tomorrow, and then I want you to come back on

Monday morning and see me again, and I'll get you to sign a contract.'

'What, the no-swearing crap?'

'That's the one—and no abusive language or threatening behaviour. No doubt you've heard it all before. Right, come with me and I'll get you your methadone for today and tomorrow,' he said, and to be sure, he dispensed it himself.

There was only enough to last the man for a couple of weeks, so he'd have to order more. Not surprisingly there wasn't much demand for methadone in the sleepy little town of Butley Ford, and he imagined they kept a small supply for just this sort of contingency.

He went back into his room, gave it a quick squirt of air freshener and called in his first patient, apologising for holding her up. It was the last thing he needed today, of all days, he thought, but he didn't allow himself to think about Tango until all his patients were finished. Then he shut the surgery, making sure it was properly secured in view of their latest resident, and headed for the veterinary surgery.

Maisie was just leading Tango into the surgical prep room when he arrived. Kathy showed him in, and he gave Maisie a tight smile.

'Any change?' he asked, looking down at Tango searchingly.

'Unfortunately, yes. It's still swelling. I'll knock her out, X-ray it and then we can have a good look without hurting her.'

They lifted her onto the table, and Maisie was conscious of James's eyes on her and his almost silent

huff of disapproval. Tough. She didn't have time to
worry about James and his over-developed sense of
protection where her baby was concerned. She was
fine, and as long as she could do her job, she'd do it.

She gave him a level look, and he raised a brow
and backed off, folding his arms and regarding her in
grim-lipped silence.

Until they'd shaved Tango's foreleg.

'What anaesthetic will you use?' he asked.

'Thio—thiopentone—to knock her down, and then
Isoflo mixed with oxygen to keep her under.' She hit
the vein first time, to her relief, since James was
standing over her breathing down her neck, and the
first thing she did once Tango was out and Kathy was
happy she was stable was move her jaw very carefully
to test if there was any resistance from the joint itself
to indicate a dislocation.

There wasn't, and so she inserted an airway and
secured it, then took an X-ray of the dog's head. Well,
to be exact, she retreated from the room and Kathy
took the X-ray. She wasn't that stupid. It took only a
few moments to develop, and it was frustratingly in-
conclusive.

'There are so many structures in the head it's difficult to make out one from another,' she explained
to James. 'I think I can see something here, though—
just a vague outline of something that might be an
abscess. Right, Kathy, let's turn her on her back and
have a look.'

They tied her limbs out onto the table to hold her
steady, covered her with drapes and then opened her
mouth wide, securing it.

'Oh, yes,' Maisie said. 'Look—here, on her palate,

on the left side, right up near the joint. And it's obviously tracked up towards the back of her eye. Right, I'll open it up, take out what I can and look for a foreign body, but I may well not find anything.'

'What sort of foreign body? A splinter?'

'Or a thorn. Anything like that which has caused a penetrating injury resulting in infection. There may be nothing there at all, just a septic puncture wound. Is she right out, Kathy?'

Kathy pinched Tango between her toes, and nodded. 'Yup. Nice and stable. She's looking fine.'

'Good.' Maisie sliced open the abscess, removing the pus and checking it for splinters and thorns, but there was nothing. 'Rats. I was hoping to find something. Right, I'm going to go a bit further in, to try and find out why it's affecting her eye.'

'Do you think the splinter might have gone up further?' James asked, and she shrugged.

'I have no idea. I hope not. If I open it up so it can drain, hopefully it'll start to mend and her eye will go down, but it's bound to swell further with all this poking about. I don't want to damage anything, but if I'm not thorough enough, it could just flare up all over again.'

And then, to her relief, she found a tiny shard of wood, almost rotted away, soggy and soft but obviously enough to have caused the damage.

'There you are,' she said, holding it up. 'Your splinter.'

She hadn't realised how tense he'd been until she saw his shoulders drop.

'Thank you, Maisie,' he said quietly, and she threw

him a smile and carried on. She wanted to rinse out the area with saline, then leave it to drain.

'I won't give her antibiotics for twenty-four hours, until we're sure all the pus is out and it's on the mend, because otherwise you get pockets of pus sealed in and it just comes back.'

James leant back against the wall and crossed his arms, and his smile was crooked. If she hadn't known better, she would have thought that his legs were shaking.

'No doubt you'll help me keep an eye on her.'

'Of course. Right, let's wake her up.'

Tango came home at three, still a bit wobbly on her pins, but James had never been so glad to see a dog in his life.

'You just didn't want to tell your sister you'd killed or blinded her dog,' Maisie teased, and he nodded agreement and wondered if she realised just what a pushover he was for a pair of light brown eyes.

Canine or human.

They tried to encourage her to lie in her bed, but she didn't want to know. She staggered over to the sofa, climbed on, leaving one back leg behind, and flopped down with a big sigh. Seconds later a soft snore drifted from her, and he laughed quietly.

'So much for the bed. I might have known it was a waste of time.'

'She should be fine now. She probably won't eat today, but you could offer her water, and if she keeps it down you might try her with some boiled rice and chicken, very sloppy and cut up tiny, and just a very small amount at first.'

He nodded, then looked at Maisie. She was tired, he realised, her lovely sparkle absent, and she should have been resting. Instead, she'd been operating on Tango, and probably saving her sight, if not her life.

A lump came to his throat, and he swallowed it. 'Thank you, Maisie,' he said, but the lump was still there and his voice was gruff.

And then, just because he couldn't help himself, he took her in his arms, dropped a light and fiercely controlled kiss on her soft, surprised mouth, and hugged her.

CHAPTER EIGHT

IT WAS only gratitude, Maisie told herself.

Maybe if she said it enough times, she'd end up believing it, but her stupid, hopeful heart wouldn't give up, and she spent the night in turmoil.

Because, of course, she'd realised in the brief seconds of that kiss that she loved James—truly loved him, in the lay-down-her-life-for-him sort of way that had never hit her before, but it had hit her then, with the force of an express train.

Did he love her? Was that why he'd kissed her? She didn't know. All she knew was he'd said something about her needing to rest, and hustled her out of the door with what had felt like undue haste but had probably been more to do with her reluctance to leave his side for even a minute.

So here she was, on Sunday morning, taking the dogs for a walk and wondering if she'd bump into him. Of course, she had the perfect excuse to go round there and check on Tango, but she didn't want to use it. She wanted him to come to her, perversely, but he didn't, and she didn't meet him on the river wall, and it was only when she thought to check her answering-machine that she found a message from him.

'Hi. Tango's looking a bit better. Thanks for everything you did. I imagine you're walking the dogs. Fancy coffee? I'll be in all morning.'

Except, of course, it was almost twelve by the time she found his message, and she'd been moping all morning.

Idiot. She went round, tapped on the door and opened it. 'James?'

His voice came from the depths of the house. 'Hi. Come in.'

She went through the scullery and kitchen and found him buried up to his armpits in a packing chest in the hall. 'Lost something?' she said, feasting her eyes on his long, straight legs and taut buttocks as he bent over the box. What she wouldn't give for the right to go up to him and lean over and slide her arms around his waist...

'Oh, just some stuff of my sister's. She rang me, asking about it.' He straightened up, ran his fingers through his rumpled hair and shot her a smile that nearly blew her socks off. 'Morning.'

'Good morning. I see Tango's eye's gone down.'

'Mmm.' He looked down at the dog, studying her as she stood between them, her tail waving and her eyes fixed devotedly on him. Maisie could understand that. He crouched down and stroked her gently, and she took a couple of steps towards him and licked his chin. 'So—are you happy with her?'

And, of course, Maisie had to go close to see Tango, and that meant being right beside him, their legs touching as she crouched and looked at the dog's eye more thoroughly.

'Yes, I'm happy,' she said, and met his eyes. 'She'll be fine, I think. I'm pretty confident the danger's passed and her eye's safe.'

He nodded. His gaze stayed locked on hers, and for

a moment she thought he was going to say something, but then he stood up and turned away.

'I'll look for Julia's stuff later. Come and have a coffee.'

And that was it, the opportunity for him to lean over and kiss her good morning gone, wasted.

So it had been just simple gratitude, she told herself, the kiss last night nothing more complicated than that.

Damn. She swallowed the bitter regret and followed him through to the kitchen. There was a jug of coffee on the go, and he poured them both a mug and handed hers to her. They sat at the end of the big refectory table, and not for the first time Maisie wondered what on earth a bachelor was doing with such a huge table. The bulk of the antiques she could understand, but the kitchen table?

'My great-grandfather won this table at cards,' he said suddenly, as if he'd read her mind. His finger was tracing a little spill of coffee, doodling in it on the polished surface, and a smile flickered at the corner of his mouth. 'It caused havoc when it was delivered to the house in London. My father remembered it arriving, and the cook was so incensed at the huge thing in her kitchen that she flounced off and they had to manage without her till she calmed down. It took a week or more, apparently.'

Maisie laughed. 'I love it, but if you put it in my kitchen I might flounce. I wouldn't be able to walk round it, especially now. I'm getting huge.'

'What are you? Twenty-one weeks? That's over halfway.'

She nodded. 'I feel good now, though. Much better.'

'Good.' His smile flickered again briefly and was gone, and he started fiddling with a card that was propped up between the salt and pepper in the middle of the table. For a moment he frowned at it, then he shot Maisie a thoughtful look. 'Fancy going to a wedding?'

'A wedding?'

'Mmm. A friend of mine in London's getting married in two weeks. I have to go, and I was going to take Jools—my sister—but she won't be here. I wondered if you fancied coming.'

There was something he wasn't telling her, she thought, so she asked him.

'Why me?'

'Why not?'

She shrugged. 'Because when you turn up with a pregnant woman in tow, tongues will wag.'

He stared at her, as if she'd just said something extraordinary, then grinned. 'They will, won't they? What a wonderful idea. So—will you?'

'Only if you tell me why,' she said, standing her ground, and his grin became wry.

'My ex is going,' he said simply, and her heart crashed against her ribs.

'Ex?' she echoed, and he nodded.

'We were together for five years. I was happy in general practice, she wanted to go and save the world. She thought I was pandering to a load of spoilt and pampered capitalists, and she wanted me to go and save the children of Africa.'

'What, all of them?' Maisie said, wondering why

he hadn't gone, because if she knew nothing else about him, she knew he had a soft heart.

He laughed, then his smile died. 'Pretty much. She couldn't see that helping a woman cope when her baby was crying all night and she was worried sick about money and her husband was drinking it all could in any way be valid. I disagreed. It may not be cutting edge save-the-world stuff, but it's no less important, and I know what I do can make a difference.'

'So she dumped you and went to Africa to save the children?'

He gave a short, bitter laugh. 'No. I left her, just over a year ago, around the time my father died, and she prostituted her principles for a merchant banker. Still, he's probably better in bed than me.'

I doubt it, she thought, and then coloured hotly when she thought she'd said it out loud. Not that she knew, of course, and that kiss had been nothing if not chaste, but even so...

'Sorry. I'm just a bit raw about it, but in fact she did me a favour, because otherwise we probably would have got married—'

'You weren't married?'

He shook his head. 'No.'

'Oh.' Relief coursed through her, for no good reason, and she smiled. 'I just thought, when you said ex...'

'Just a figure of speech. So—will you come?'

'As a human shield?'

His smile was wry. 'I don't want her feeling sorry for me, or thinking that the road's open to come back to me, because it isn't. I'm happier now than I've been for years, and I feel settled here. I could put down roots, Maisie, real roots. I spent the happiest days of my childhood in this little town, and I want to stay here. And Carla would hate it.'

Maisie thought of the looks she'd get, the whispered remarks, some maybe more direct, and then thought of having James to herself all the way, all day long and all the way back.

No contest, really. 'Yes, I'll go with you,' she said rashly, and wondered if she'd regret it. 'So long as you don't mind all the gossip from the other people.'

He cocked his head on one side and looked at her quizzically. 'Why should I mind?'

'Because they might think it's your baby?'

A strange expression flickered in his eyes and was gone. 'Let them think what they like. I'm not ashamed of you, Maisie—far from it—so provided you don't mind if people think it's mine, we could give the society mill something to grind. It might be fun.'

Fun. Suddenly it seemed like ages since she'd had fun. 'I've got nothing to wear, of course,' she said, and he laughed.

'Women always say that.'

'But under the circumstances I think you might believe me,' she pointed out fairly, looking down at her steadily growing bump, and he grinned.

'I believe you. You do have a decent excuse, I suppose.'

'Will I need a hat?'

'Probably. Does that make you happy?'

She laughed, realising that it did. 'I am a woman, you know,' she said lightly, and again that strange light flickered in his eyes.

'Of course,' he said. Dropping the card onto the table, he stood up and poured his coffee down the sink. 'Sorry, I have to find this thing for Jools. Thanks again for looking after Tango. Don't forget to bill me.'

And that was that.

Dismissed, she took herself back to her house, studied her wardrobe and realised that she quite literally didn't have a thing she could wear. She'd been wearing her jeans and work trousers with the top button undone, but that was beginning to be insufficient and her shirts were gaping now because of her slowly swelling breasts.

She needed everything from the skin out, she realised, and there was only one person who liked shopping enough to cope with that. She picked up the phone.

'So what brought this on?'

'Apart from the fact that bits of me have gone up two sizes? I've got to go to a wedding in London with James.'

'What? You jammy thing! When? How? Why?'

'Two weeks—just under—and apparently it's fairly dressy, so I'll need a hat.'

'Great,' Kirsten said, cutting them both another slice of fruit cake and curling up on her sofa, eyes alight. 'You really need to choose the dress first, I suppose, and you can't have a big brim or anything too clumpy, you'll look like a mushroom with a fat stalk.'

'I feel so much better for knowing that,' Maisie said drily. 'So when are we going to do this?'

Kirsten looked at her watch. 'It's two-thirty. The shops shut at four on Sundays. We've got an hour and a half—bit less. Come on. No time like the present.' And getting up, she took the cake away from Maisie before she could take so much as a bite, and dragged her to her feet.

In fact, it was easier than she'd imagined. They went to a large department store, looked in the maternity department and found a wonderful dress in a silk and linen mix. It was pale green, almost pistachio, and in the winter it wouldn't have suited her, but because she'd caught the sun it looked gorgeous.

'I'll need a strapless bra,' she said doubtfully, and Kirsten shrugged.

'I'll lend you mine. I'm bigger than you, but it'll probably fit you now. Right, hat.'

And there, perched on top of a hat stand in the millinery department, was a delicious little concoction of pale green feathers.

'How appropriate,' Kirsten said with a grin, and plonked it on Maisie's head. 'Fabulous. What do you think?'

She turned her head, the feathers shimmering artfully over one eye, and chuckled. 'It's crazy.'

'It's a summer wedding. It's perfect—the colour couldn't be better. Buy it.'

So she did, mourning the fact that it represented at least one kitchen unit, but she hardly ever went out anywhere smart and she just felt like being silly.

And, besides, she didn't want to let James down, and if people thought they were together...

'Shoes.'

'I've got shoes. I've got some strappy sandals that

will do,' she said, refusing to blow the whole of her kitchen budget, James or not, and anyway her legs were aching.

'Right. Let's go back and finish that cake,' Kirsten said with a grin.

'Right, I want your assurance that you're going to abide by the letter of this contract,' James said. 'Are you sure you've read it and understood it?' He'd gone over the contract with the addict anyway, just to be on the safe side and because he wasn't sure how good the man's understanding was, but it was Monday morning and, as predicted, Lenny's craving was making him twitchy. He was so desperate he would have signed anything.

'Yeah, yeah, I understand. Just give me the damn stuff.'

'First things first. Sign here,' James said, trying not to breathe in as he leant over towards Lenny and countersigned it in front of Jane.

The contract was the usual one they had in the practice, Jane had told him, and should prevent any abuse of privilege.

Should. However, James had his doubts. The man was definitely strange. Nobody in their right mind got their face tattooed, in his experience, and there was something about the wild eyes and nervous twitching that made him very, very uneasy.

'Right,' he said, and ushered Lenny through to the reception area for his daily dose of methadone. To his relief the usual dispenser, Elizabeth, was on duty, and he handed the prescription to her, and also a copy of the contract.

'He knows the rules. No abusive language or threatening behaviour, or we refuse to dispense the methadone—and that's not just to staff, but to other patients. Any trouble, I want to know straight away,' he said, as much for Lenny's benefit as Elizabeth's, and went back to his room, squirted the air freshener round it again and called in his next patient.

Over the next week and a half, Maisie's bump grew much more noticeable. She had an antenatal appointment with Jane Shearer on Friday afternoon, the day before the wedding, and of course they were busy at the veterinary surgery, but at least they had their locum now, a lovely girl called Jenny, and, as David had predicted, Pete had fallen heavily under her spell.

'Could you cover me so I can go to my antenatal?' she asked Jenny, and she'd been given a willing smile in return.

'Sure. How are things?'

'Fine,' she replied, and physically, of course, it was true. It was only emotionally she was a little at sea, and that was all her own stupid fault. She kept thinking about that kiss James had given her—the meaningless one that she couldn't seem to get out of her sad, desperate little mind—and she was wondering if the romantic atmosphere of the wedding the next day would help things along.

She was still thinking about the wedding as she parked in the car park of the doctors' surgery in Butley Ford, and so her mind wasn't really on what she was doing as she walked towards the entrance.

If it had been, she might have seen him coming, but as it was the knife was pressed against her throat before she had time to register his presence. All she could feel was an arm around her throat, the prick of the knife on her neck and a choking, vile smell of unwashed body jamming in her throat.

'What—?'

'Shut up! Just shut up and get inside!' he snarled, and propelled her none too gently towards the door. He kicked it open and it slammed back, bouncing off the wall and ricocheting into Maisie's arm and making her cry out.

Behind the desk she saw the elderly receptionist's eyes widen, and seconds later James was there.

'I want my stuff,' the man said, and James nodded.

'OK, Lenny. Let her go and we'll talk about it.'

'No. I want it now. You gave me some other crap this morning—it tasted funny. It wasn't the same—you're trying to trick me, but I know!'

'OK, Lenny. Just let her go, could you, and I'll get it for you. Just let her go first.'

'No. I want my stuff.'

'You have a contract,' James said, leaning idly against the wall and studying his fingers as if he didn't care one way or the other if the man got whatever it was he wanted. Drugs, Maisie realised, and felt the knife move away from her neck.

She started to sigh with relief, but then felt the prick of the knife lower down, against her abdomen, and her eyes widened with fear.

'Touch that child and I'll break your neck,' James said mildly, and she could see the steel in his eyes.

'I don't believe you. Get me the stuff.'

James straightened away from the wall. 'If you hurt her or the baby, you'll never get the drugs. Now, which is it to be, a long wait in a police cell on a murder charge, or let her go now and I'll give you your dose? Which is, after all, why you're here, isn't it?'

She felt his grip loosen. 'How do I know you aren't lying?'

'You don't,' James said. 'But you're getting nothing like that. What have you got to lose?'

And that was it. She was free, running towards James, thrust behind him into the safety of the office while he twisted the man's arm up behind his shoulder and the knife fell to the floor with a clatter.

'Ow, you're hurting me!' Lenny whined, but James just smiled grimly.

'Sorry,' he said, not looking in the least repentant, and his eyes scanned over Maisie briefly, their expression unreadable. 'You OK?'

She nodded, wondering if her legs would give way. 'Yes, I think so.'

'Right. Stay there. I'll just find out what happened this morning, and I'll be with you.' His grip tightened. 'Right, Mr Price. Come with me.'

James felt sick with relief. Lenny was gone, hauled off by the police after he'd had his methadone, and Jane had taken Maisie gently away and pronounced her unharmed. She was sitting in Jane's room drinking a cup of tea with her now as her antenatal clinic was over, and as he joined them he was trying to get the image of Lenny with the knife at Maisie's throat out of his mind.

Not that there weren't plenty of other things to think about. They were dealing with another dispensing error. It had been obvious to him the moment he'd clapped eyes on Lenny that he was suffering withdrawal symptoms. He was sweaty, shaking, agitated and probably even more unpredictable than usual, and he'd complained the stuff he'd had that morning had tasted funny.

And when James had unlocked the cupboard at the bottom where the methadone bottle was kept, he'd found it empty, and beside it, in an almost identical heavy amber glass bottle in the same stock size, was temazepam elixir. Similar green syrupy liquid, only instead of the heroin substitute, Lenny had been given a sleeping draught.

The normal dose was five to ten millilitres, and Lenny had been given thirty, enough to send the average person to sleep for days, but Lenny, of course, was not exactly an average person and, as he'd confessed cheerfully once he'd had his methadone, he'd had temazepam before so it was no big deal, and he hadn't had to pay for it this time.

'At least the bastard won't sue,' James said to Jane, but his main preoccupation wasn't relief that they'd escaped a major disaster with this latest dispensing error, but that Maisie was all right. When he'd seen Lenny hold the knife to her throat, he'd felt sick with fear for her, and when Lenny had moved it down to threaten the unborn baby, his rage had nearly overwhelmed him.

'Sue? He'd better not try, after that stunt,' Jane said fiercely.

'He seemed to think getting the Temazepam was a bit of a laugh—a freebie on the National Health,'

James told them heavily. 'When I think what might have happened...'

He was thinking of Maisie, but Jane was clearly still concentrating on the dispensing error and the repercussions it might have had. 'We'll have to submit a report and instigate an inquiry,' she said. 'And you know who was on this morning?'

'I can guess. Is she all right?'

'Not really. I've sent her home she was so distraught. I'm not sure if it was the knife or the knowledge of what might have happened if someone else had taken that which worried her so much. I'll drop in and see her on the way home, make sure she's OK.'

He nodded, then his eyes flicked to Maisie's. 'Are you really OK?'

She nodded. 'Yes. I was just a bit shaken. I'm fine now.'

He swallowed and looked away before he made a fool of himself. 'Good. I'll take you home.'

'I'm fine. You've got a surgery.'

'It'll keep for a while if necessary. Are you sure you're all right?'

'Yes—really. I'm sure.'

James wasn't. He wanted to undress her and run his hands over every inch of her body, checking it for cuts and bruises and signs of harm, and kiss better every one he found.

Just as well, then, that he did have a surgery. 'I'll see you later,' he said as he showed her out. 'And don't be afraid. He's in police custody, he can't harm you, and we don't have any other addicts on the books at the moment. I'll come and see you on my way home.'

'James, I'm fine,' she said softly, and, rising up on tiptoe, she pressed a fleeting kiss to his lips and left. He watched her go, then turned to find Jane's speculative eyes on him.

She nodded slightly, then with a little smile she turned back to her room. 'I've got to be off. Will you be all right this evening?' she asked.

He followed her back into her room and closed the door. 'I'll be fine. What about Patsy?'

'I've called Elizabeth and asked her to cover tonight and tomorrow morning, because I think until we can get to the bottom of this, we'll have to suspend Patsy. We can't let it happen again.'

'No, we can't. We'll lose our dispensing licence, not to mention our reputations. Will you have time to see her?'

'Yes, I— Oh, damn! Oh, no. James, we're out again tonight.'

'I'll see her,' he said, cursing the fact that he couldn't do what he wanted to do and go straight round to Maisie's house and take her in his arms. Perhaps it was just as well. 'Where does she live?'

'Just down the road from you—the little terrace on Rectory Road. It's one of the middle ones, the one with the porch.'

He nodded. 'I'll find her. You go. Are you sure you're all right for tomorrow?'

She smiled at him. 'I'm sure. You go to the wedding and have a lovely time with Maisie, and forget all about this. It'll do you both good.'

It was seven-thirty before he got to Patsy, and he found her tearful and still beside herself with anxiety.

He tutted gently at her and led her back into her living room, sitting down on the sofa with her and holding her hands as she wept and tried to explain, almost incoherent.

Almost. One word stood out, though. The word 'blind'.

He took her chin, tilted her face up to him and stared into her eyes, searching for the clouding of cataracts and finding nothing, then sighed softly and let her go. 'Patsy, how long ago did you notice that you couldn't see as clearly?' he asked gently.

Her shoulders lifted in a tragic gesture. 'I don't know. I realised about a month ago that I couldn't really see clearly enough to drive, so I stopped. It's only the middle bit of the picture, though, if you know what I mean. My left eye's been funny for a while in some lights, but just recently the right one's been sort of fuzzy, too. Usually it's all right, but there's something about the light in the dispensary—have I got cataracts?'

He shook his head. 'No. I think you might have a condition called macular degeneration, and if you have, that could explain why you're finding it hard to read labels, because it affects the centre of the visual field only.'

'And am I going to go blind?'

He shook his head. 'I don't think so—not if I'm right. And the progress of this thing can be halted with laser surgery, too, in certain cases, so there's more hope than there used to be for it. The first thing is to refer you to an ophthalmic surgeon for a thorough examination, and then some decisions can be made. But in the meantime, I don't think you should be working with medicines,' he said, gently but un-mistakably firmly.

'But who will do it?' she said, wringing her hands. 'I knew I couldn't see that clearly, but I thought, so long as I didn't make a mistake, I could keep helping out. Then there was that young girl with her penicillin, and now this—and when I saw that horrible, horrible man threatening to stick a knife in Miss McDowell's baby and it was all my fault—'

'Don't,' James said, trying not to think about it himself. 'Don't torture yourself. She's all right, thank God, and so is Lenny, for which we all need to be profoundly grateful. Just now he's sleeping off all the excitement in a police cell, and Maisie's OK, so there's no harm done.'

Except to my blood pressure, he added to himself, and when he'd calmed Patsy down a little more, he left her with a firm instruction to come into the surgery on Monday morning and see him so he could examine her more thoroughly and refer her to the hospital specialist.

And then, without any further ado, he went round to Maisie's and found her curled up on her sofa with all three dogs surrounding her, fast asleep. He tapped on the window, and she woke with a start and sat up, eyes wide.

He saw the moment she realised it was him, and told himself he'd imagined the flash of joy on her face.

It was relief, that was all—relief that it was him and not some random axe-murderer or junkie come to cause havoc with her life.

She opened the door to him, and he folded her against his chest and hugged her.

'Are you really all right?' he asked, his lips pressed to her hair, and she nodded and snuggled closer.

'I was so scared,' she confessed, and he remembered, not that it was ever far from his mind, that it was the second time in five months that she'd been assaulted by a man. He got his emotions firmly under control and then lifted his head and searched her wide, guileless amber eyes for clues to her emotional state.

'Will you be all right to go to the wedding tomorrow?' he asked softly, and she smiled her heartbreakingly lovely smile and shook her head at him in reproof.

'Of course I'll be all right. I'm looking forward to it. Have you eaten? I've saved you some supper because I thought you'd probably work late. It's in the fridge—it's only quiche and salad, and there's some crusty bread.'

It sounded wonderful, he thought, not least because it meant he'd get to sit and eat it in her company—and tomorrow he'd have her to himself all day.

Suddenly things were looking up...

CHAPTER NINE

THE wedding was wonderful. It was held in the beautiful and very ornate upstairs function rooms of an old pub right on the Thames, and sitting beside James during the warm and informal marriage ceremony with the river as a backdrop to the bride and groom brought a huge lump to Maisie's throat.

If only, she thought, but put her sentimental thoughts on hold and concentrated on doing what she was supposed to be doing—being a human shield to protect him from the beautiful and elegant and infuriatingly slender Carla.

The meal was wonderful, the group of people at their table great fun, and to her surprise she found herself thoroughly enjoying it. It was hot, though, and towards the end of the evening they stood on the balcony over the water and sipped mineral water instead of champagne, because James was driving and she didn't want to drink because of the baby. They caught the slight breeze coming up the river and watched the lights come on in the trendy apartments opposite as the sun went down.

The breeze fluttered the feathers in her hat and they tickled her face, and James laughed at her, teasing her about it and saying he'd always known she was a bird fancier, but his eyes said something quite different.

At least, she thought they did, but she wasn't sure, and up to now he'd been nothing but polite and friendly, attentive to her every need and yet keeping that infuriating distance that she didn't know how to erode.

But now, with the meal and the speeches over, the jazz quartet who'd played throughout the wedding cleared away their things and a DJ took over, playing all the cheesy old songs that brought a lump to her throat or made her want to sing along, and everyone was moving onto the dance floor.

Would he dance with her? Probably not, she thought regretfully. Too intimate—although, of course, if they were to give the impression he'd moved on, he would have to—unless he used her pregnancy as an excuse.

Very likely. But even so, although she'd managed to convince herself he wouldn't dance with her, she found herself swaying unconsciously to the music and watching the other couples longingly.

James noticed it, of course, and raised a brow. 'Want to dance?' he asked, and she nodded.

'If you do.'

He sketched a little bow and held out his hand, his mouth quirking into that wonderful smile, and she placed her hand in his and let him lead her to the floor. He took her in his arms, not close, like the others, but holding her at a respectable distance, until she wanted to scream.

Then the music slowed, becoming unmistakably sexy and romantic, and someone bumped into her from behind, pushing her into him. She felt him sigh softly against her hair, fluttering the little feathers against her cheek as he drew her closer to him, one arm sliding down to rest gently in the small of her back, the other cradling her hand against his chest as he swayed slowly to the music.

She laid her head against his shoulder and closed her eyes. He was a wonderful dancer. His movements were smooth and sensual, his sense of timing impeccable, and she found herself wondering what he'd be like as a lover.

No. Crazy. She'd drive herself mad thinking about things like that. If she wasn't careful she'd forget that she was merely there as a decoy, to throw Carla off the scent and make her think James was moving on with his life.

Which he was, of course, but just not with her.

More's the pity.

James closed his eyes and rested his cheek against Maisie's hair, careful to avoid the crazy little hat, if you could call it such a thing, and wished things could be different.

Every now and again he felt the baby move, sometimes a kick, sometimes a wriggle, and it brought a huge surge of protectiveness washing over him. Every time he closed his eyes he saw Lenny holding a knife at Maisie's throat, and he had to stop himself crushing her against him. She'd been so brave about that, and she'd been wonderful today.

She'd smiled and laughed and talked to all his friends, and had avoided saying anything which gave away their true relationship, so that all of them were left guessing.

And all of them adored her.

All but one, he thought, and then there was a tap

on his shoulder and he lifted his head and met Carla's eyes.

'Can I borrow you for a moment?' she said, and Maisie looked from one to the other, smiled at him and moved out of his arms.

'I could do with sitting down again,' she said graciously, and left them to it.

And Carla, the woman he'd thought he loved, the woman he'd once thought he'd marry and have children with, moved into his arms and he couldn't believe how wrong she felt.

'So, this is really it for you, isn't it?' she said, and suddenly he realised he couldn't lie to her, of all people.

'Yes, it is,' he said, then added honestly, 'It's not my baby, though.'

'Doesn't matter, does it? Funny how love just broadsides you without warning,' she said, and smiled understandingly at him. 'I'm glad you came. I've got something to tell you. I'm getting married, James— to Will.'

Extraordinarily, he felt nothing. 'Your merchant banker?' he asked.

She nodded, then her smile faded. 'Don't be angry with me about the Africa thing. I suppose I just wasn't in love with you, and I wanted an emotional challenge. I'm sorry I said all those things to you. I didn't really mean them, you know. I am proud of you, and I know what you do is good and makes a difference to people's lives. I was just bored, and we were going nowhere. I just didn't realise it.'

He smiled down at her, understanding her absolutely. 'Don't worry. You did me a huge favour.'

She smiled back fondly. 'I can see. I've never seen you look as happy as you do tonight.'

Was he looking happy? How odd. He shouldn't. He was marking time, waiting for a time when he could say something to Maisie, and somehow it just didn't seem appropriate, not while she was carrying another man's child.

'Good luck,' Carla said, and taking his face in her hands she kissed him. 'For old times' sake,' she murmured, then moved out of his arms and out of his life, going back to her Will, and he could see the sparkle in her eyes when she looked at him, and he knew it was right for her, too.

He found Maisie on the balcony, not sitting, as she'd said, but standing staring out over the water, a far-away look on her face.

'Are you OK?' he asked softly, and she turned and smiled up at him, but the smile didn't really reach her eyes and he realised she was tired.

'I'm fine.'

'Are you ready to go?'

'If you are.'

He nodded, and they said their goodbyes, using the baby and their journey back to Suffolk as their excuse, and then he was driving through the still-busy city streets, cutting through the suburbs and then out into the dark velvet night.

Maisie was asleep beside him, her lashes dark against her cheeks, and he drove carefully, his protective instinct at full throttle. It took two hours to get back, and he pulled onto her drive and cut the engine. She didn't stir.

'We're back, sleepyhead,' he said softly, and her

lashes fluttered up and she looked up at him, all disorientated and unfocussed, and he had an unbearable urge to lean over and kiss that soft, expressive mouth. Instead, he forced himself to get out and go round and open the door for her, helping her to her feet.

'Ouch,' she said, getting out of the car without her shoes, because her feet were sore from teetering about in strappy bits of nonsense. Without hesitation he scooped her up in his arms and carried her, giggling, to the door, her shoes dangling from his fingers behind her back.

'Key,' he said, and she found her key and slipped it in the lock and opened the door, and he carried her over the threshold with a strange feeling of unreality.

Wasn't that what the groom was supposed to do to the bride? And yet it hadn't been their wedding, so why was he even thinking about it?

He set her down, sliding her slowly down his body, feeling the solid fullness of her pregnancy against his body as she found her feet at last.

The dogs were milling around their feet, having been fed and walked and spoilt by Kirsten, who was no doubt waiting in the sitting room for Maisie. It was probably just as well, James thought, because with Maisie's soft unfocussed eyes staring up at him he wasn't at all sure he'd trust himself alone with her.

'Thank you so much for such a lovely day,' she said with that beautiful smile, and his heart crashed against his ribs.

'Any time. Thank you for coming with me. I really hadn't been looking forward to it, and having you there made all the difference,' he said honestly, and then, because he just couldn't stop himself, he bent his head and touched his mouth to hers.

Her lips softened and parted, and the invitation was almost too much for him, but with a superhuman effort he pulled away and straightened up.

'Goodnight, Maisie,' he said firmly. Calling Tango, he handed Maisie her shoes, walked out of the door, put the dog in the car and drove round the corner to his house. Then he sat in the kitchen and downed a hefty slug of single malt before making his way upstairs.

He didn't put on his bedroom light, just crossed to the window in the dark and watched for her bedroom light to come on. It didn't, and he realised she was probably having a cup of tea with Kirsten downstairs.

Yes. He could see her crossing the room, a mug in her hand, curling up on the sofa.

'Hell, you're stalking her, you're as bad as Stevenson,' he said. Disgusted with himself and frustrated beyond belief, he shut the curtains firmly and went to bed, and dreamed that it had been their wedding and the baby was his, and when he woke to Hector's dawn fanfare and the dream faded, the sense of loss was like a crushing weight on his heart.

'Idiot,' he told himself, and vowed to keep a greater distance, for both their sakes. Starting right now with a run along the river wall, he thought, and, pulling on his shorts and trainers and a fresh T-shirt, he clipped on Tango's lead and headed down the drive.

At least at five in the morning he wasn't likely to bump into her!

*   *   *

James was glad to get back to work on Monday morning and have something else to think about.

Patsy came to see him, as instructed, a little more composed but still very frightened of the repercussions of her dispensing errors, and he realised she was more concerned about that than about the fact that she was going slowly and inexorably blind.

'Lenny Price is OK,' he was able to reassure her, 'and Elly's ear's better, so I don't think you need to worry. It's not incompetence or carelessness, it's a medical problem. Now, you were saying on Friday that you find it's worse in some lights than others,' he said, and she nodded.

'The cupboard at the bottom, with the methadone and temazepam, is very dark, and the methadone was virtually finished. There was only the tiniest dribble in it, so I used the next bottle. They seemed just the same—I can't believe I didn't check the label more closely, but the bottles were identical and I just assumed we'd got more than one on the go.'

'Perhaps we should look into positioning them differently,' he said, 'but don't worry. That's another matter. I'm only concerned now with your health.'

To start with, he looked into her eyes with an ophthalmoscope, but it wasn't really conclusive. 'I can't really see clearly enough to diagnose anything,' he said, 'so I want to refer you to a specialist who can have a closer look at your eyes and find out if it is macular degeneration or some other condition. If it is, it means that the part of your retina responsible for your central vision is starting to fail, for one reason or another. There are two types of macular degeneration, wet and dry, and he'll probably inject some dye—fluorescein—into your veins and look into your eye to see which sort it is. That will help him decide what form of treatment, if any, you can be given, but I have to warn you, Patsy, there may not be anything very much that can be done to improve it, although there are new treatments being developed all the time which may be more effective at halting the progress of the disease.'

'So will I go blind?'

'Probably not. If it is macular degeneration, and I'm fairly certain it is, you'll gradually lose more and more of your central vision, although it can be a very, very slow process, and you'll usually retain your peripheral vision so it's more frustrating than anything. I'm really sorry.'

She shook her head as if to clear it. 'I knew something was going on, but I can still read, in the right light. I suppose that will go.'

'Eventually, probably.'

'Oh, dear. I do so love to read.' She sighed and gave him a shaky smile. 'Still, it could have been so much worse. Are you going to press charges against me?'

'Press—? Absolutely not, Patsy, but we may have to consider what you can do in the surgery so no vital mistakes of any sort are made because you haven't been able to read something clearly.'

She shook her head. 'No. I can't see well enough to be safe, Dr Sutherland, not doing such important work. I couldn't bear another mix-up. I'll leave. I'm sixty-two. It's time I went. I'll just take up knitting. I can do that without looking, and there's always the radio and talking books when it comes to that. I'll manage, don't you worry about me.'

And she went out, leaving him frustrated because there was nothing he could do to help her. Or, at least, not enough. He'd hand her care over to the specialist and hope there was something he could do to slow or halt the progress of the condition.

His surgery finished, he tapped on Jane's door and filled her in on the consultation with Patsy.

'Poor woman. Still, it explains a lot—not least her short temper. She's obviously been worrying about this all alone for ages. I wish she'd said something, but at least there weren't any fatal consequences.' She looked up at him and smiled. 'So—how was the wedding?'

'Lovely,' he said, and didn't bother to tell her just how lonely and frustrated he'd been ever since. Still, he'd get over it. He'd have to.

July moved into August, and Maisie found things were getting harder. Standing to operate, struggling to lift a reluctant horse's hoof and staying bent over to do a flexion test in a lameness assessment—heavens, just reaching her own feet—all of them started to become irritatingly difficult.

And James was being even more difficult.

Well, he wasn't, but she realised she wanted more from him than he was giving her, and she was frustrated and discontented because of it and that annoyed her, because it should have been the happiest time of her life and it wasn't.

She felt increasingly alone as the time of the baby's birth drew slowly nearer, and although she was really looking forward to meeting her little one, she was growing more aware of how much of the experience she wanted to share with James.

Instead, she shared it with Kirsten, who was itching to get her hands on the nursery.

'I haven't got a nursery,' Maisie said, laughing, but Kirsten was adamant.

'You'll need a nursery.'

'Not until it's born and I know what sex it is,' Maisie said, but it was nothing to do with the sex, and everything to do with not tempting fate. Like she'd felt with the house, she was still waiting for someone to tell her it was all a mistake and she wasn't having a baby after all.

She got round the problems at work easily enough. She sat to operate, and Jenny took over the equine and other large-animal work, and Pete helped her when necessary.

'So I just get to do the teeth trimming on the guinea pigs and all the cat spays,' she grumbled good-naturedly, but in fact she was grateful, because she didn't want to take any risks with her precious cargo.

David was getting better slowly but surely, and would be back by the time she needed to go on maternity leave, hopefully, especially if she worked to quite near the end.

Then she went to her antenatal class for the first time, held by the midwife in the health centre premises, and it dawned on her that she was the only one there without a partner.

Not that it mattered for the first few weeks, but during the last two classes, they were told, their birth partners should be present.

She bumped into James on the way out, and he asked how it was going.

'OK. I don't have a birth partner, though, which could make it awkward next week,' she told him, and she wondered if she sounded as forlorn as she felt. 'I suppose I could always strong-arm you into it.'

'Except that you'll probably give birth when I'm the emergency doctor, just for maximum nuisance value,' he said with a wry grin.

He sounded so reluctant she shook her head. 'Don't worry. I'll ask Kirsten, although she faints if she cuts herself. At least I'd know you wouldn't faint or do anything stupid, but you're right, you'll probably be busy and it needs to be someone I can rely on.'

But Kirsten threw up her hands in horror. 'Hell, no! I don't even want to be there when *I* give birth! Sorry, kiddo, you'll have to find someone else.'

Kathy, the head vet nurse? They didn't really have that sort of relationship. Ann, David's wife? Ditto. In fact, she didn't have that sort of relationship with anyone, she realised.

Oh, well. She'd manage. She went to the class alone.

One by one, they introduced their husband or partner, except for one woman whose mother was going to be with her. Then Eileen looked at Maisie.

'Who's going to be with you when you give birth?'

She lifted her chin and was about to announce that she was doing it on her own when a voice behind her said, 'I am.' She turned, her eyes widening, just as James strolled towards her with a lazy grin and sat down cross-legged beside her on the floor mat. 'Sorry I'm late—I was held up in surgery.'

Eileen opened her mouth, shut it again and smiled a little vaguely.

'Right. Well, at least I'll know you understand the principle of childbirth, Dr Sutherland,' she said, and then started talking about pain control in labour and the role of the partner in helping to alleviate it. The other pregnant women, many of whom saw James for their routine antenatal care, gradually stopped staring at James and Maisie with speculative gleams in their eyes and paid attention to what Eileen was saying.

And then they had to practise it, and Maisie found herself lying down as James tried each technique on her in turn.

Effleurage. Light, stroking movements over the skin, his warm palm gliding over her abdomen, soothing and restful. Back massage, with the heel of his hand firmly rubbing in the small of her back, easing the ache that was always there these days. Acupressure points for pain relief, used in shiatsu—between the thumb and first finger, for instance—and all the time his hands on her, the strong, supple fingers finding tight spots and soothing them away.

It was wonderful, she thought, relishing the feel of his hands on her body. If she closed her eyes, she could almost imagine that she wasn't pregnant and he was just touching her, the gentle, subtle movements of his massage a prelude to love-making.

But it wasn't. It was a vital part of preparation for the birth of her baby, and she needed to concentrate on it so she was ready when the time came.

But what if he was only here for this class, and not for the real thing? Would she be able to cope without him? And why was he here? She'd asked him last week, and he'd seemed so reluctant. What had changed his mind?

'Are you OK with this, really?' she asked him softly as they put the mats away at the end, and he grinned at her.

'I wouldn't miss it for the world.'

'People are going to talk,' she warned him, but he just flashed that grin again and shrugged.

'I've told you before, I'm not ashamed of you, Maisie. If they want to talk about us, let them talk. It's nobody's business but our own.'

'What changed your mind?'

Something flickered in his eyes, but he blanked it out. 'I wondered what kind of a friend would let you go through it alone,' he said after a moment. 'I didn't like the answer. So here I am.'

She swallowed and turned away. So, just a friend, then. Funny how much that hurt. 'I'm very grateful,' she said, knowing that, whatever the reason, she needed his support as much as she needed air to breathe. 'Will you be OK for next week? Because if you're busy, I'll quite understand.'

'Of course. I said I'd be here for you, Maisie, and I meant it,' he said, and she felt silly and ungrateful because she wanted more than he was prepared to give her, and that was just unrealistic. She should content herself with his friendship and not try and reach for the stars.

Knowing her, she'd just fall flat on her face.

The following week, he was back, slipping in just after the start again and taking his place beside her.

'Hi. How's it going?' he whispered, and she smiled.

'Fine.'

'Your timing's perfect, Dr Sutherland,' Eileen said with a smile. 'I want to talk about alternative positions for giving birth, rather than lying down on your back, which closes the pelvis, and you'll need your partners for this. Right, could you all stand up, please, nice and slowly, and face each other?'

And the next thing Maisie knew, James was standing in front of her, and she had her arms around his neck and was squatting, hanging on his neck, opening her pelvis to allow the baby to pass through more easily, and his hands were on her sides, helping to support her.

How could she be hanging there on his body and yet feel so supported, so secure, so...safe?

They practised other positions, squatting, leaning, kneeling—all of them involving her in touching his body in some way, feeling the support of his arms around her, the solid comfort of his chest, the sheer power of his legs braced around hers.

It suddenly all seemed very real, and she tried to imagine what it would be like to face childbirth without him.

Awful. She needed him, in so many ways, and not just for the birth, and if he kept on holding her like this she was going to break down and cry.

Don't think about it, she told herself, and after what seemed like for ever the class was over. James seemed as glad to get away as she was.

'Right, well, good luck, everyone,' Eileen was saying. 'I'm sure I'll see you all soon in clinic, either

before or after your deliveries, but, remember, what
do you have to do?'

'Breathe through the contractions!' they all cho-
rused, and laughed and filed out.

Maisie felt James's hand on her back, ushering her
through the door and walking her to her car.

'I'll be round shortly to walk the dogs,' he said,
and she nodded. She was finding walking harder than
ever now, because the join at the front of her pelvis
was softening and the see-sawing movement of walking made it ache.

Only three weeks to go, she thought as she got
home, and it occurred to her that she hadn't yet
packed her case or bought anything for the baby.

She was still at work every day, although it was
mid-October now. So close, she thought, and felt a
flutter of panic. Still, it was the weekend, she could
rest and recharge her batteries a bit.

She went upstairs to the bathroom, and glanced out
of the window. James had taken the dogs and was
heading down the lane. She watched him for a moment. It was getting dark, and he would only be able
to go a short way before the light failed completely,
so he'd probably only take them on the roads. Still,
at least the heat had passed, finally, the Indian summer coming to an end with a spell of much-needed
rain.

She lingered at the window for a minute, then was
about to turn away when she heard the unmistakable
screaming of a panicking horse. She stared through
the gloom but she couldn't see anything. She knew
where it was coming from, though. Anna's ponies at

the end of the lane—and unless she was very much mistaken, one of them was in serious trouble.

Without thinking, without hesitation, she ran downstairs, flung open the door and drove down the lane. It was quicker than walking in her condition, and there was no time to lose...

CHAPTER TEN

HE COULDN'T believe it.

James had been heading off with the dogs when he heard what sounded like a horse screaming. He'd gone back to investigate, and had nearly been run over by Maisie's car skidding to a halt outside the field.

'Put the dogs in the run and come and help me,' she yelled, clambering awkwardly over the fence and running across the field.

He did no such thing. He shut them in her car, followed her over the fence and reached the far side of the field just in time to see her grabbing a horse by the head collar and dragging it away from a gateway.

'Go on, go away!' she yelled, hitting it on the rump, and it cantered off, leaving his field of vision clear.

And what he saw made his blood run cold.

A horse had reared up and got its foreleg caught between the gate and post at the hinge end, and it was struggling violently to free itself. But that wasn't what disturbed him. The thing he found most shocking was the image of Maisie, eight and a half months pregnant, sitting on top of the gate and trying to calm the panic-stricken horse, attempting to pull the hoof up and free it all at the same time.

'What the hell are you doing?' he yelled as she

hauled up on the hoof once more, and she turned and glared at him.

'What does it look like? Don't just stand there, James, come and help.'

'No way! It's crazed with pain, Maisie. It'll kill us both!'

'Rubbish,' she said, sliding down off the gate into the other field and grabbing the horse's head collar again. 'Are you going to help, or are you just going to stand there and watch it tear its hoof off?'

'You're mad,' he said, but he realised there was nothing he could do to stop her. She was utterly focussed on the horse, trying to stop it making the injury even worse. 'How about a sedative?' he suggested, but she shook her head.

'It won't work in time. We have to free it. I want you to lift the gate off its hinges.'

He stared at her for a fraction of a second, but, realising the only way to get her out of there was to free the horse first, he grasped the gate and heaved. The horse screamed again and threw itself backwards, but with another massive wrench the gate came off its hinges and the horse was free.

Incapable of gratitude, it wheeled round and lashed out. James grabbed Maisie and dragged her through the gateway and up against his chest, shielding her with his body. 'Are you all right?' he asked, his heart hammering in his chest, but she gave him a scathing look and shrugged him off.

'Of course I'm all right. It missed me by miles.'

He let her go, searching her eyes in the gathering gloom, and she pushed him aside impatiently and went back into the field after the horse.

'Maisie, get out of there. That's an order,' he said, his fear for her making him forget, foolishly, about her independent streak. She threw him a black look over her shoulder and carried on walking.

He tried again. 'If that horse lashes out again it could kill you or the baby.'

'It won't lash out again.'

He didn't believe that for a moment, and he ploughed on relentlessly. 'If you don't care about yourself, at least have the common sense to look after your unborn child.'

She stopped then, but only to turn and glare at him once more. 'Yes, *my* unborn child,' she said, her voice coldly furious. 'Remember that. It's *my* baby, James, not yours. Just because you're going to be my birth partner doesn't give you any rights over me, so you might bear that in mind when you're throwing your weight around. I know what I'm doing, and if you've got nothing useful to offer, then back off and leave me alone. I'm not a complete idiot.'

'You could have fooled me,' he growled, stunned by the ferocity of her attack. 'Are you coming out of there, or do I have to come and get you?'

'Are you deaf? Watch my lips, James. I said back off. There's an injured horse in this field, and I intend to catch it and treat it. If you don't want to help me, feel free to leave.'

But he wasn't free. He couldn't leave her, because she'd get herself kicked and trampled and he'd never be able to live with himself. So he stayed, and helped her catch it and lead it, hobbling on three legs, over to the fence where the lights from her car would illuminate its foreleg well enough for her to see the injury. He passed her things through the fence in grim-lipped silence until she was satisfied that the limb wasn't broken and she'd done all she could.

And then a car pulled up and a woman leapt out. 'Maisie? My God, what's happened?'

'Oh, hello, Anna, I'm glad you're here. It's OK. Bruno got caught in the gate but I think he's all right.' She straightened up, wincing a little, and met James's eyes defiantly.

'We'll be all right now if you want to go.'

He didn't. He wanted to drag her away from the horse and put her into a warm bath and rub her back, and hold her close and tell her how his heart had nearly stopped when he'd seen the horse lash out, but he couldn't, because, as she'd been kind enough to point out, he had no rights over her.

'Feel free to leave,' she'd said. Well, now he was, so he took Tango from her car and walked the short distance to his home, his heart still pounding and her words echoing in his ears.

My baby, not yours.

'How about *our* baby, Maisie?' he whispered, and felt the sharp sting of tears in his eyes. Damn. He was an idiot to have expected anything else, after all she'd been through. He poured himself a small shot of single malt with hands that shook uncontrollably, and downed it in one.

She could have been killed. She, and the baby that wasn't his, snuffed out just like that by a pain-crazed horse out of control.

'Bloody little fool,' he muttered, the tears scalding his eyes, and he blinked them away angrily and went upstairs to his bedroom. He could see the field from there, and he watched her as she finished off and then drove slowly home up the lane.

He ought to go round and check on her, he thought, but she'd only bite his head off. What she probably needed more than anything now was rest. He'd leave her alone. That was what she'd asked for, and it was the least he could do.

Great theory. He kept it up for an hour, in which time he glowered at the bottle of malt but resisted it and had coffee instead, but then his concern for her overrode his reluctance to interfere where he was so obviously not wanted, and with a growl of self-disgust he yanked open the door, to find her there on the step, a soft bag in her hand and her eyes filled with pain.

'James? I'm sorry. Can you take me to hospital? I think I'm having the baby.'

And as she stepped inside, her eyes widened and she looked down at the spreading pool of amniotic fluid at her feet.

'I think you could be right,' he said gently. Putting aside his own pain, he drew her into the kitchen, took off her coat and sat her down at the table his great-grandfather had won at cards. He crouched in front of her and took her hands in his, and noticed they were trembling.

'I'm all wet,' she said, sounding astonished.

He felt his mouth twitch. 'You are,' he agreed, but he was relieved to see that the amniotic fluid was clear and there was no blood or meconium in it, and no odour.

He'd been reading up on his midwifery since she'd asked him to be her birth partner, and it had all come back to him. Not that it was ever very far away, but it didn't hurt to brush up.

'How frequent are your contractions?' he asked, and she looked puzzled.

'Frequent? I don't know. I thought they were Braxton-Hicks'. I've been having them for days—weeks.'

'And have they changed?'

'Yes,' she said wryly. 'They hurt now.'

Just then she gasped and her eyes widened, and he looked at his watch, then reminded her to breathe, slowly and steadily, then more lightly as the contraction strengthened, then deeply again as it faded.

'Wow,' she said, her eyes slightly glazed. 'That was amazing. The breathing worked.'

'Good.' He kept an eye on her face as he retrieved his shoe from behind the sofa cushion where Tango had hidden it earlier, then started hunting for the other, but before he could find it she had another contraction.

'That was two minutes,' he said, and as realisation dawned he abandoned his search for the shoe. There was no way Maisie was going anywhere tonight.

'What are you doing?'

'Phoning Eileen. I'm sorry, Maisie, you're having this baby here, whether you like it or not. There isn't time to move you. Your contractions are too close together and I daren't risk taking you.'

'Here?' She felt panic rise in her chest. 'But I have to get to hospital,' she said. 'The baby's not due yet. What if something goes wrong?'

His mouth tightened. 'We'll just have to make sure

it doesn't, and you're thirty-seven weeks. That's fine.
It's perfectly viable without support by now.'

'Are you sure?'

He crouched down in front of her again, the phone
in his hand, and looked steadily, reassuringly, into her
eyes. 'I am a doctor, Maisie. I do know what I'm
doing.'

She looked away, suddenly ashamed because of the
way she'd spoken to him in the field, but it had only
been because she'd been afraid, both for herself and
for the baby, and she'd known he was right.

'I'm sorry I yelled at you,' she said, looking back
at him, and hurt flickered in his eyes before he
masked it with a smile.

'Forget it. Eileen? Hi, it's James Sutherland. Look,
Maisie's gone into labour, and she's progressing fast.'
He was silent for a moment, listening, then his eyes
flicked to Maisie's and away again. 'No, I haven't
examined her, but her contractions are two minutes
apart and her membranes have ruptured. No, that's
what I thought.'

Another silence punctuated by cryptic remarks, and
then he put the phone down slowly and looked at her,
his eyes assessing.

'Is she coming?'

'She can't. She's at another delivery—the woman
from your class who wasn't there tonight. She's about
to give birth, and Eileen can't leave her.'

'So what about me?' she asked, not liking the
sound of that one bit. The panic escalated. 'Who's
going to deliver me?'

'Apparently I am.' He gave her one of those quicksilver smiles of his, but it didn't quite reach his eyes. 'You've got me, Maisie—all to yourself.'

He was a doctor, for God's sake! He knew what he was doing. He just had to call on his professionalism and get on with it.

'Stay there,' he ordered, as if Maisie was going anywhere. He ran out to his car and brought in his bag and a delivery pack that he kept in the boot for emergencies.

'I've had another one,' she said, and he wondered if he had time to get her upstairs, never mind to hospital.

'Come on, I'm taking you up to bed,' he said.

'Finally,' she said, and for a moment he wondered what she meant. No. Crazy idea. She'd told him to go to hell not two hours ago.

He took her to his room and covered the bed with clean towels and another sheet, then covered it all with the plastic-backed paper sheet that was in the pack.

'Right. You need to get out of those clothes,' he said, shooing the dog out and closing the door. He could be professional, he told himself as he helped her undress, he could—but when the last garment came off and she stood in front of him, naked and very gloriously pregnant, a huge lump the size of a house jammed in his throat and he could hardly speak.

She was beautiful. Beautiful and ripe and—bruised, for heaven's sake.

There was a mark on her hip, blue and purple, just starting to come out, and she looked down at it in astonishment. 'What's that?'

'I don't know, but it's hoof-shaped,' he said meaningfully, and the urge to shake her was only margin-
ally overwhelmed by the urge to take her in his arms
and crush her to death.

He did neither. Instead, he led her to the bed and
helped her climb up on it, then threw her a clean
T-shirt from his drawer. 'Put that on so you don't get
cold,' he ordered, and went and washed his hands.
Out of habit he snapped on rubber gloves, then took
a steadying breath.

'I have to examine you, Maisie—make sure everything's all right.'

'OK,' she said, but her voice was tight and she
didn't meet his eyes.

That was fine. He didn't want to meet hers either,
because if she saw what was in them she'd probably
run a mile. She'd told him exactly where he stood
earlier, and now was not the time to get into how he
felt about her.

'You're almost fully dilated,' he said, and as he sat
down on the bed beside her, her eyes widened and
she grunted.

'I've got to push,' she said, her voice urgent, and
she started to struggle up from her sitting position.

He held her still with firm, gentle hands. 'No. Not
yet. You're nearly there, Maisie. Just hang on.'

'But I need to push.'

'No, you can't. Not yet. You'll damage your cervix
and hurt the baby.'

'The baby, the baby, always the baby!' she yelled,
kneeling up and glaring at him. 'What is it with you
and this baby? You've spent my entire pregnancy telling me what I can and can't do because of the baby!

Don't pull the horse out of the river, don't lift the dog onto the table—what about me? What about not doing things because they'll hurt *me*?'

'But I said—'

'Oh, you say all sorts of things, but I'm sick of listening! I'm sick of hearing you being reasonable! Do you have any idea how frustrating and hurtful it is being in love with you and knowing that you just think of me as a pregnant *friend*?'

She spat the word as if it was poisonous, and he stood there, his mouth open in shock, staring at her in awe as she continued to harangue him.

'When I met you, I thought you were gorgeous. Then I realised you're wonderful as well, and I stupidly went and fell in love with you. But you never meant me to, did you? You were just being kind, looking after me, because that's all that's in your job description—looking after Maisie. Well, to hell with looking after me! I don't want you to look after me. I want you to love me, to want me, not have to put rubber gloves on before you can bring yourself to touch me!'

She ran out of breath and slowly, deliberately, James stripped off the latex gloves and dropped them on the floor.

'Marry me,' he said, and she stopped dead in the middle of another tirade and stared at him.

'What did you say?'

'I said marry me. I love you, Maisie. I've been in love with you since you yelled at me about Tango, or maybe even earlier, since you got lemonade all down your front and blushed when you realised your T-shirt had gone transparent. I don't have to wear gloves to bring myself to touch you. I've spent the last five months keeping myself firmly in check because I find you so beautiful and so desirable. I want you, Maisie, more than you could ever imagine—you and your baby. I want to marry you, and have a family with you, and grow old with you—if you'll let me.'

She sat down with a plop on the bed, her labour temporarily forgotten. 'You love me?' she said, her face stunned, and he reached out a fingertip and lifted her chin, closing her mouth.

'Yes,' he said softly. 'I love you.'

And because there didn't seem to be anything else as urgent to do, he drew her into his arms and kissed her.

Seconds later she broke away, her eyes widening.

'Can we talk about this later?' she panted. 'It's just— I really do need to push now.'

She gave birth twenty minutes later, to a lusty, squalling, healthy little girl, and James lowered Maisie to the old bed in which generations of his family had been born. Lifting the T-shirt out of the way, he laid the baby against her breast. Instantly she turned her head, rooting for the nipple, and found it, latching on without hesitation. It was the last straw for him.

'Congratulations, Maisie,' he said unsteadily. 'You've got a beautiful baby daughter.'

She stared down, her expression rapt, and he moved away, giving her room to meet her baby in private. The love on her face was more than he could take, and he turned away, staring blindly out of the window and across the dark, windswept marshes.

She hadn't answered his question, he realised. He still didn't know if she'd have him, if she'd marry him.

'James?'

He turned, meeting the amber eyes still filled with love, and she smiled and held out her hand to him. 'Come and say hello to her,' she said, and he walked back to her, his legs shaking like jelly, and sat down beside her before they gave way.

'Hello, baby,' he murmured, touching her palm with one finger and feeling that wonderful response as the tiny little fingers gripped his fiercely and hung on. Then he lifted his head and met Maisie's eyes again. 'Well done,' he murmured. 'You did really well.'

She was still smiling, her eyes shining with love and happiness. 'I think we make a pretty good team,' she replied, then he saw doubt flicker in her eyes. 'At least—I think we do. What you said earlier...'

'About marrying you?'

She nodded. 'Did you...' She swallowed. 'Did you mean that, or were you just cheerleading?'

He chuckled softly and, hitching himself up on the bed beside her, drew her into his arms. 'Cheerleading? No, Maisie, I wasn't cheerleading. I've never been more serious in my life.' His smile faded. 'I meant every word. I love you, my darling. I love you, and I can't imagine life without you, but the choice is entirely yours.'

Relief flooded her eyes. 'Then—yes, please,' she said, a smile blooming on those beautiful, kissable lips. 'I'd love to marry you. Besides, I think we should, don't you, for the sake of your professional reputation? Or do you intend to escort all your patients to childbirth classes? In which case I might have something to say about it.'

He laughed and hugged her carefully. 'I don't give a monkey's about my professional reputation, as far as you're concerned. There's nothing that having you in my life in any capacity will do but enhance it. I've told you over and over again I'm not ashamed to be associated with you. I'm proud of you, Maisie—proud and very, very much in love with you, despite your headstrong independence. And, no, I don't intend to escort all my patients to childbirth classes, so you can relax.'

She laughed, then her face creased slightly in concentration. 'I think I can feel another contraction,' she said, and he eased her out of his arms and stood up.

'In which case,' he said, 'I'd better finish this job.'

They looked up at Eileen as she walked in an hour later, bag in hand, and took in the scene at a glance.

'Better late than never,' James said with a lazy grin.

'Everything all right, Dr Sutherland?'

He smiled at Maisie, then looked back at the midwife. 'Yes. Everything's fine, thank you. Absolutely perfect.'

'And has he been looking after you all right, Maisie?'

Maisie returned his smile, her eyes still on her soon-to-be-husband. 'Absolutely. Looking after me is what he does best. In fact, he's so good at it, I'm going to let him do it for the rest of his life.'

And James, because he didn't want to be found derelict in his duty, bent over and kissed her again…

EPILOGUE

THEY were all clustered in the kitchen—her husband, his sister Julia and Julia's new fiancé, Ann with David, fully recovered now, Pete and Jenny, looking increasingly like an item, Jane and her husband Michael, Eileen, the midwife who'd arrived like the cavalry when it was all over—and Kirsten, sitting at the kitchen table with the baby in her arms, looking for all the world like a besotted godmother.

Funny, that, Maisie thought with a smile.

It had been a wonderful day. They'd decided to do it all at once, and so they'd had a double ceremony, their marriage and the baby's christening, because all the same people would be there and it seemed silly to have two ceremonies in quick succession.

There were others, too—Carla and Will, and a few of James's London friends, and old friends of hers from vet school—and it had been a wonderful day.

The dogs, of course, were loving it. They were wandering around under everybody's feet, vacuuming up the crumbs and looking hopeful, and Julia, absolved of any guilt for abandoning Tango and going to live in Australia with her new husband, was busy fussing over the dog and spoiling her rotten.

Suddenly an arm snaked round Maisie's shoulder and she found herself being steered out of the kitchen and into the old scullery.

'James!'

'Shh.' He pushed the door firmly shut behind him and drew her into his arms, and she went willingly, laughing up at him.

'What are you doing?' she asked, and gasped as he drew her harder up against his body.

'It's my wedding night. I've waited long enough to get you to myself.'

'James! It's only mid-afternoon and we're in the scullery!' she said with a little shriek, but he smothered it with his mouth, warm and coaxing, teasing at her senses until her body flowed against him.

Then he broke away. 'Come on,' he said, a wicked smile in his eyes, and she felt a bubble of laughter rising in her throat.

'Where?'

'The Lodge. We'll sneak round and go in the back way.'

'But I haven't got the key, and it'll be freezing!'

'No, it won't. I turned the heating up—and I've got the key.'

He dangled it under her nose, and together they crept out of the back door and ran round, scattering Helga and the now fully grown chicks as they dashed through the gate into the garden of the Lodge.

His fingers fumbled the key, and he swore softly and tried again, then stopped her as she went to go inside, scooping her into his arms and carrying her over the threshold. He lowered her to the ground, sliding her down his body so she could feel every intimate part of it.

'Do you remember when I did this after the wedding?' he said, his voice gruff, and she lifted her hand and cradled his cheek.

'Yes. I wished it had been our wedding, that it had been real. And you kissed me, but then you pulled away.'

His brow creased. 'I had to, Maisie. I wanted you so badly. Dancing with you—'

'Dance with me now,' she whispered, and led him through to the sitting room. She put on her favourite romantic CD, and then turned into his arms. 'Dance with me,' she said again, and with a ragged sigh he eased her closer, lowered his head and covered her mouth with his.

A lifetime, she thought dreamily. I've got him for a lifetime. And there was another life inside her, a life he didn't know about. She'd tell him later. Just now, there were other things to think about...

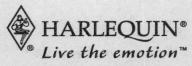

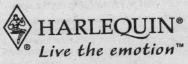

Harlequin Romance®

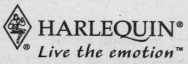